Inimical

M.J. Flare

ISBN: 978-1-5356-1356-9

For Hito

"They say only the good die young
That just ain't right
'Cause we're having too much fun
Too much fun tonight"

-Lana Del Rey

Acknowledgements

INIMICAL COULD NOT HAVE BEEN made possible without the constant support of those around me. I want to start off by thanking my partner in crime, David, for putting up with my constant nagging of him to read every chapter I typed. As sad as the book got for him at times, he continued to push through it no matter how upsetting the story got.

I would like to thank one of my best friends, Destiny, who let me name a character after her. Same goes for Jauni! Two awesome girls that are part of my life and deserve such recognition.

My proofreaders! Those who read *Inimical* before anyone else, giving me input and suggestions. Thank you, Celina, Edgar, Andrea, Vanessa, Diana and my older sister, Stephanie. Though Stephanie liked *Inimical*, she couldn't help point out that I "chose some names." But thank you for your ongoing support and loving criticism.

Also, my little sister, Elvira, who even though was at a young age when I finished *Inimical*, she was really so intrigued by the plot that she decided to read it on her own. Now that's mature!

To my other mothers, Felicia, Ida, and Mary, who always gave me support no matter what I chose to do in life. I couldn't have gotten back on my feet after falling if I hadn't had your help. I also would like to thank my college buddy Douglas, who kept telling me to just go for it and publish. That push went a long way!

Contents

I

Siege

BUZZZ. BUZZZ.

I awoke to the sound of my phone vibrating. I hadn't realized I'd even fallen asleep. I sat up on my bed and rubbed my eyes. How long was I out for? I reached over to the table at the side of my bed to retrieve my phone. I had one unread message.

Zanniel, your father and I have work to do at the office and won't get done until later. We might not make it home in time to say our goodbyes before your flight. Have fun at Jason's tonight and call us when you get in. We love you.

They love me? Some parents they are. They can't even take off work for a few hours to properly say goodbye to their only son before he leaves the state to go to another college. Whatever. My flight wasn't until 10:00 tonight and it was barely 5:30. They could come say goodbye if they really wanted to.

I didn't even want to go to Jason's. Out of all my friends, *he* was the last I thought would ever be the one to get married, to settle down. I hadn't talked to Jason in the past few months. I was kind of surprised when he called to tell me the big news. His wedding was tomorrow but the rehearsal dinner was tonight, my last day in Albuquerque.

I've weighed out my options the last couple of days as to what to do. I could go to his dinner thing, make my one last appearance, say goodbye to everyone, then board my flight and never look back. Or I could just ditch the dinner and leave everything behind without saying a word to anyone. Either way, I had to leave. I needed a change to my life—nothing excited me here anymore. New Mexico was big, yes, but it was too small in its own way.

My freshman year at the university here wasn't anything to brag about. Popularity was fun to a certain extent, but after a while it started to feel like a chore. I hated that everyone knew who I was. I had brains, looks, talents, everything any teenager would need to be at the top of the popularity list. High school was a breeze, and my first year of college was beginning to feel the same way. I was on a basketball scholarship, a full ride. Not that I needed the money; my parents were loaded. I did several sports throughout my years in high school but I decided to stick to only one athletic program. For my first year, anyway.

I had joined a fraternity as well: Sigma Pi. Needless to say, it was nothing like they make it seem in the movies. We did more volunteer work than anything—it started to feel like having a job. The parties that were thrown weren't even parties at all; they were a gathering of a few people, some snacks, the music set to low, and little to no alcohol. I didn't even have to rush or pledge or even prove myself worthy of being one of them. I basically just walked into the building and I was already accepted. My fraternity brothers also didn't treat me as an equal. They felt the need to get cleared by me for anything they wanted to do. They came to me for answers when something wasn't right. Worst part of all, they looked to me for guidance, which was a little pathetic considering about half of them were seniors and I was only a freshman. Smooth and flawless as my first year was at the university, I hated almost every minute of it.

I needed to get out of here. As soon as basketball season ended, I began to look at other campuses in different states. I did a few campus tours before I finally made my choice: the University of Kentucky. It was perfect. I would start fresh, make new friends, start a new life, and maybe, just maybe, I could move on from everything tying me down to this place. It would be my perfect escape.

BUZZZ. BUZZZ.

My phone vibrating brought me back from my thoughts. My friend Tristan was calling.

"Hey," I answered.

"Hey," he replied. "There's a sour tone. You ready to go to Jason's?"

I sighed. "Yeah, I'm not sure if I want to go, dude. My flight's in a few hours and I want to make sure I get everything I need. You know, double check."

"What?!" I could hear the disappointment in his voice, "you packed like a week ago. You're all set. Come on, you can't leave us all without saying goodbye."

I knew it was pointless to argue. In a way, I *did* want to go to the rehearsal dinner but not for Jason. I wanted to make one final appearance before taking off. It sounds selfish and cocky but no one in this city, or state, was at my level. Everyone was below me in more ways than one and I wanted to leave one last impression of the only good thing that ever happened here: Me. And Tristan was right—I was all set. "I'm not even ready, dude. I just woke up before you called me."

"It's cool, I'm not ready either. The dinner starts in like an hour. I'll go to your place and we'll get ready there. We'll take my car there and I can drop you off at the airport when we're done. Sound good?"

"I guess." It was convenient having Tristan live down the street from me, not even five minutes away. "Okay, I give. I'll go."

I could have made him beg me a little longer to go but I decided against it. I almost ended the conversation when I remembered something. "Hey, I forgot to tell you—you'll never guess who I ran into today at UNM."

"Who?"

"Satchel. It was the weirdest thing, I had gone earlier to pick up a copy of my transcript and when I was on my way to the parking lot, he was leaning over my car. Like he was waiting for me or something."

Tristan went quiet. Neither of us had seen Satchel in the longest time. He was the brother of a friend. A lost friend: Fletcher. We never talked about the incident. I thought it would be best to just let it be and continue with our lives. As messed up as that sounds, it was for the best. No sense to mope around carrying the memory of an old friend, wondering what it would be like if he was still alive. Why burden yourself with that? Talk about torture. I had a different way of seeing things, and in a way, I gained the respect of others by it.

A few beats passed and he hadn't said a thing. "Tristan?"

"Wait," he finally said. "Satchel Jarvis? Fletcher's brother?"

Was he serious? "Do you know anyone else in this world named Satchel?"

"When did you see him? W-w-what did he tell you? What did he do?"

There was an edge to his voice, almost seemed nervous. "Not much." I got up and went to my closet and began looking through clothes. "Just asked how I've been and was wondering if there was anything I wanted to tell him."

"What did you say to him?"

"Said I've never been better. He looked awful, dude. Like he hadn't eaten or slept in days."

"And then?"

He sounded eager for more. "Then… I asked him why he didn't attend his own brother's funeral. Kind of messed up if you ask me."

Tristan went quiet again. "I'll tell you more when you get here. I'm goin' to shower."

"Okay," he said, "I'll leave now."

The call ended. He was more nervous about Satchel than I was. Did Tristan see him, too? Hmmm… Whatever, it's not like it mattered anymore. I didn't see anything in my closet that looked appropriate enough to wear to a rehearsal dinner. All my good clothes were already packed and I wasn't about to go dig something up.

I went to my dresser and froze when my eyes came across an old picture frame from junior year of high school. It had a photo of me and all my friends huddled together in our basketball jerseys. I was in the middle, of course, to my left was Tristan and to his left was Jason and our other friend Kalvin. To my far right was Clemont, Nolan was to his left, and between him and to my right was Fletcher. My body had tensed up and I realized I was holding my breath.

I relaxed my shoulders and picked up the picture frame and held it up to get a closer view. As I looked at the expressions of everyone I realized how happy we all were. Not a care in the world. None of us could have expected that we would lose Fletcher our senior year. I stared at Fletcher for a few beats. Memories began rushing to my mind of everything we had gone through. We did every sport together, we practically lived at each other's houses, we never really argued about anything, we were so… happy.

I shook my head and freed myself from all those thoughts. I remembered the reason why I hadn't packed the photo. It had too many memories, too much sorrow that I didn't want to follow me. I set the frame back down and headed for the bathroom.

I decided to take my shower first and then continue to look for clothes. As I was getting cleaned up, I began to get excited about Kentucky. I had originally gotten a basketball scholarship to that university as well before I started my freshman year here. I don't know what I was thinking back then—I was stupid not to have left. My new life could have already unfolded. But I wasn't going to waste any more time. After tonight, my new life would begin.

I got out of the shower and just threw on a black hooded sweater vest and some jeans. I would wait to see what Tristan was going to wear and go on from that. I wiped the mirror clean from the steam of the shower and started to do my hair. I got a bit of hair wax and ran it through my bronze hair to give it volume. Once I finished my hair, I stared at my reflection for a few moments. I was thankful to have gotten my mom's hazel-colored eyes. I don't know whose eyebrows I inherited but they were never satisfying. So thick and never a good appeal. I wasn't a fan of facial hair so I always had a clean face. I looked pale, but still looked good as ever.

I was brushing my teeth when I heard glass shattering coming from my room. I rinsed my mouth and headed to my room. As I entered, the picture frame I was just looking at was on the floor, broken. How did it fall? I had placed it back where I had it, and that was nowhere near the edge. Strange. I took this as a sign, so I picked up the broken frame and tossed it into the trash along with the picture I chose to leave behind. I picked up the broken glass and tossed the pieces into the trash as well.

I went downstairs to wait for Tristan. Not long, before I even sat down on the couch, I saw headlights flashing through the living room windows. It was already starting to get dark outside so the lights were blinding. I went to open the door and shouted out, "Come upstairs!"

I went back upstairs to my room to look at my remaining options of clothing one more time. I could hear footsteps coming from the hallway.

"I don't know what to wear, dude," I began. "All of my good stuff is already packed." I turned around as I heard him come in. "What are you going to—"

I stopped mid-sentence. "Are we…crashing the dinner?"

I took in what Tristan was wearing: black pants, black hoodie, and a white mask with silver duct tape over the mouth in the shape of an X. He didn't say anything, he just stood there.

I was confused. "I don't get it—what's with the mask?" I couldn't see his eyes. It looked like he was wearing sunglasses behind the mask.

No response. "Whatever then." I turned away. "Look, if you want to crash Jason's dinner, that's all you. Call Clemont or Nolan or whoever, but I'll pass."

BUZZZ. BUZZZ.

My phone vibrated in my pocket. I pulled it out and I had one new message… From Tristan.

Hey, I couldn't find my keys. I'm on my way now.

I felt a cold shiver run down my spine. I read the message over and over trying to make sense of it. If Tristan was barely leaving his house, then who…?

I turned around to find an empty doorway. Whoever was standing before me was gone. I was frozen in place. I could feel my heart begin to race. Was this a prank? Why would Tristan want to play a prank now of all times? Assuming of course that this *is* Tristan who was just in here. I took a tentative step forward. Then another. I searched all my surroundings and did a double take when I looked at my dresser. The broken picture frame that I had just tossed in the trash was now sitting back in its place. My eyes widened. Who was just here? And why were they wearing a mask? I eventually made my way outside my room and into the hallway. I looked around and still saw no one.

I let out a sigh. This had to be a prank. Ha-ha, Tristan—very funny. I got on my phone and dialed his number. It rang a few times then went to voicemail. I hung up and tried again; still no answer. Damn it. I went to the bathroom, turning on all the lights as I went. There was no one here. But I *saw* someone here.

Just then, all the lights in my house went out and I was standing in complete darkness. I held my breath and stood still, listening closely for any noise of movement. I breathed out when I heard nothing after a few beats. I turned on the flashlight setting on my phone and used it as a guide as I walked back out to the hall. I wanted to call out but I didn't know what to say. Hello? Who's there? I remembered watching horror movies and criticizing the victims being terrorized for asking stupid questions.

I heard a car approaching then saw a new set of headlights come to view as they illuminated parts of the living room. I stayed upstairs and waited. I looked around and decided to get the baseball bat from my room. Thinking of horror movie victims, *I* wasn't going to be one. If I needed to defend myself from anything, at least I had some sort of weapon.

"Zanniel?!" I heard a voice call from the outside—it was Tristan's voice. I heard the door open and saw Tristan rushing in. "Zanniel?" he called again. He was out of breath. I was confused, so it wasn't Tristan's car that had pulled up earlier. Granted, the lights were on high and couldn't see what kind of car had arrived or who was even driving it. I had assumed it was Tristan since he was the only one I was expecting. Okay, poor choice making in my part. But that cleared up one doubt: Tristan wasn't the masked one that I saw in my room.

"Up here," I called back.

He looked up and met my eyes when I flashed the light in his direction. He sighed with relief. "That's a good sign. You okay?"

Now I was definitely confused. "Why wouldn't I be?"

He opened his mouth to say something but no words came out. He was like deer caught in the lights. Did he know something I didn't? He looked around as if he was to find his answer somewhere.

"Tristan, what's going on?" I began to feel irritated. I hated when other people knew something I didn't, and Tristan *definitely* knew something. He was never a good liar—I always caught him on whitest of lies.

"I…" he tried, "I…"

He looked scared. I pointed my bat toward him. "You what?"

The lights from outside illuminated his face. The anxiety and desperation were all over it. He was still for a moment and finally said "We need to go."

I don't think he was talking about Jason's dinner anymore. I wanted more details. Why was he so freaked? *I* was the one who just saw someone in a mask in my house. There was something he wasn't telling me and I was going to find out before anything else happened. "No."

"Dude!" he pleaded, "we need to go!"

I saw a shadow move across the headlights. "Who else is here?" I demanded.

The figure that was moving outside made its way to the front door. Before I knew it, the person in the mask I had seen earlier rushed toward Tristan. I began to shout but my scream got caught. Someone came up behind me and clamped their hand to my mouth and grabbed me by my waist with the other. I dropped my bat and my phone, and began kicking and struggling as I got picked up only to be thrown down the stairs. I tumbled down the stairs, hitting every part of my body on my way down. I knew I had hit the bottom of the stairs, but the room felt like it was still spinning. There was a ringing in my ear that it made it hard for my eyes to focus once I tried to open them.

I got on my hands and knees once I managed to focus my eyes. I looked in front of me and saw Tristan on the floor. He was face down on his stomach. I couldn't see his face but he wasn't moving. I crawled my way toward him, gasping for air. Once I reached him, I shook his shoulder only to see there were splashes of blood beneath him. Was Tristan dead?

What was going on? Who was doing this? I looked around and before I could see anyone, I felt someone's hand pull me up by hair to my feet. Though I should have been in a serious pain from falling down the stairs, my body was numbed with adrenaline. I acted quicker than my attacker expected me to. I turned around and elbowed him in the face. I could tell it was a guy behind the mask because I heard him grunt with pain upon my impact. He immediately let me go. I kicked him on his side and as he leaned over in pain. I picked up a lamp on the side of the couch and smashed it over his head. He collapsed to floor and I turned to get away.

I was limping toward the door when another masked figure came from outside and rushed toward me head-on and knocked me down. I got my breath knocked out of me as I hit my back. This other masked attacker straddled its legs over me and pinned my hands toward the ground. I kicked and squirmed but he was overpowering. Assuming it was a guy as well, no girl was this strong. With one blow of his fist to my face, everything went black. I thought I was knocked out but I was drifting in and out of consciousness. When my eyes managed to focus, it looked like the masked guy on top of me had a syringe in one hand inserted to a small bottle on the other. He was extracting some substance from it that I could only guess was meant for me.

My eyes landed on its belt which had a hunting knife, or buck knife, whatever it was, clipped on to it. I don't know how I managed, but I took advantage of him being preoccupied with his hands and snatched the knife and inserted it into his right thigh. He dropped the syringe and the bottle and screamed out in pain as he rolled off me. A guy's voice once again.

My entire body was now throbbing with pain. I began to crawl toward Tristan again, trying to grab on to whatever I could do give me some sort of support. I could taste blood in my mouth. I looked around for my phone but it was nowhere in sight. Then I remembered, I dropped it upstairs before I was thrown down. I needed it—I had to call the police, call an ambulance. I needed help. I wasn't sure if my body could handle getting me back upstairs but I had to try.

I finally reached Tristan and when I turned him over, he had a blank expression on his face. His eyes were staring forward, mouth open and body stiff. Tristan was dead. My hands began to shake. Who would want to kill Tristan? I turned and saw the first attacker was out cold, the second was whimpering by the door and now a third figure with the same mask was standing in the open doorway.

I didn't move and neither did the masked figure. He just stood motionless with his hands by his sides—assuming this one was a guy just like others. Part of me wanted to believe this was a random act of violence. But the other part of me knew better. Tristan wanted to tell me something but got attacked before I could get anything out of him. He knew something was up, and had he been able to tell me beforehand, we might not have been in this situation at all.

I managed to stand up. I wasn't sure what parts of my body were broken or sprained. Everything was in pain. My eyes darted back and forth, looking around for something to defend myself with but there was nothing. My body was too weak from previous attacks—I didn't think it could handle another one. I had no energy to run and no words to speak. I had nothing. The figure looked around at the floor and I felt like he was searching for something. Was he looking for the syringe that the other attacker had? His head stopped moving when I realized he found what he was looking for and my thoughts were correct. He began walking toward the syringe so I took this to my advantage and began to limp away.

I knew I wouldn't get far but I had to try. I tried to pick up the pace but it was no use. Before I knew it, I was being pulled back by hood. I tried to fight back but I had no energy left. I felt something stab my right forearm before I got thrown to the floor. My arm was burning in pain. When I looked to it, I had the syringe I had seen earlier inserted in me. Whatever substance was in it was now rushing through my veins. I reached over and yanked it out. After I tossed it, I couldn't move. I felt my throat tighten and my body began to spaz out. The last masked guy leaned over me as I tried to catch my breath. I wanted to reach up and remove the mask to see a face but I couldn't. I stared into the dark holes of the mask, looking for eyes. But before I could find a pair, I blacked out.

II

Boundaries

I AWOKE WITH A JOLT. I sat up and looked around but failed to see anything. Wherever I was, it was dark. Well, dark at first. My eyes adjusted as I looked around me. Where was I? Some kind of room? Not too big from what I *could* see, and there was nothing else in here besides me. Then I remembered the masks, the attackers, Tristan… Last thing I remember, I was in my house. I remembered the syringe I had been injected with but I looked at my arm and saw nothing. Faintly but still visible, there was no indication of anything on my arm or my whole body. I wasn't in pain anymore. I couldn't feel anything as a matter of fact.

I stood up to better inspect my body. Not a bruise, no blood, not a single scratch was on me. Weird. In front of me was what appeared to be a door. Not a regular door with a knob but a wide door with a handle on the bottom. Sort of a garage door. Maybe a storage space? I looked around once more and saw no other alternative but to try and open it.

As I took a step forward I noticed how quiet it was. The sounds of my footsteps echoed and my breaths were louder than they'd ever been. I placed both hands on the handle and pulled it up revealing the outside. The door slid up and the sound of metal scraping against each other seemed to be louder than necessary. This reminded me of those quiet nights where the smallest noise would sound like it was ten times as loud as it normally should be.

The outside didn't have much to look at. A strange haze or some type of fog surrounded everything, making things difficult to make out. I squinted to get a better look and realized I saw more doors. They were arranged next to each other and expanded to the left and the right. I turned around to the sliding door I had come out of and concluded that I was in some sort of storage unit. All the black doors looked exactly alike with numbers on the top to identify each unit. The numbers on top of mine were 58. Not sure if that held any meaning.

Where was I? How did I get here, and why was I here? So many questions and no answers. Well, if I had no answers then I was going to *find* some answers. But where? How? I could walk down the path in between the units, but that didn't seem the smartest choice, considering I hadn't the slightest idea of where I was or what I would find. I could stay here and wait to see if anything interesting happens. Hmmm…no. I couldn't just stay here.

Okay, I'll go. But where? To my right or to my left? I couldn't tell which direction would lead me to anything helpful since it was hard to see anything more than a few feet in front of me. I decided to go the right. I walked down the path slowly at first, then I picked up my pace to regular walking strides as I saw that there was nothing more than just units. The numbers did seem to go down, though. 56, 54, 52…

I stopped in front of unit 50. I pressed my right ear to the door to see if I could hear anything from the other side. I waited and listened for a few moments but heard nothing. I looked at the black door from top to bottom seeing no difference whatsoever from its neighboring doors. I grabbed the handle at the bottom and tried to pull it open but it wouldn't budge. It seemed stuck, or locked. Hmmm… That didn't help. I banged on the door a few times and the knocks echoed down the pathway a few beats. Still nothing.

I carried on the same path I was on and didn't stop to check any of the other doors. I had a feeling that none of them would open either. I kept walking and began to wonder what would happen or what would I encounter when the numbers reached their end. 38, 36, 34...

I tried to convince myself that this was a dream. But then again, dreams had a different feeling to them. No, this must be something else. Okay, what do I know... Name is Zanniel, I'm nineteen years old, I attend the University of New Mexico, and I live in Albuquerque. Okay, my memory *was* working. Now I just had to concentrate. If this was a dream, I wouldn't even be thinking of those facts. Dreams from what I remember were like a story. Everything was planned and I had no control of my actions. This, however, was entirely different. I'm completely aware of my surroundings and what I'm doing. 26, 24, 22...

Tristan, the masked intruders, the attacks... Parts of that night were slowly creeping up on me. They seemed to flash in my memory in no particular order, and I found it hard to put meaning to any of them. 18, 16, 14...

We were attacked. But why? By who? The last time I was awake, I was in my house. Which means someone or something must have brought me here. Then again, I ask, why? 6, 4 and 2. Across from unit 2 was unit 1 and in between them both was a chain-linked fence. It had a lock in place which prevented me from swinging the door open. The top was not much higher than my shoulders so I decided to climb over. Once I got to the other side, I looked back to see a sign above the fence that read "Tijeras Self Storage".

Tijeras? I was in Tijeras? Tijeras was a few miles east of Albuquerque going toward the mountain areas. What in the world would I be doing here? I knew where I was but I couldn't be more lost. Man, was *I* far from home. How did I end up here? More and more questions continued to fill my head and I wasn't any closer to answering any of them.

I looked at the road in front of me and knew I could probably walk back to Albuquerque. But with the haze, or smoke, or fog, or whatever this thing was in the air, it was hard to see which way would lead me there. I thought it best to go with my gut feeling again. At this point, I didn't feel like I had much to lose. I turned and walked to the right.

Nothing strange caught my attention. Then again there wasn't much to see. I've driven by Tijeras a few times with my friends whenever we would go up to the Sandia Mountains. Tijeras had no inhabitants but trees, dirt, a couple of houses, and a few locally owned businesses. I walked in the middle of the road, paying close attention to anything that didn't belong. So far, nothing looked out of place.

As I walked, I began thinking of the flight I was supposed to be on to Kentucky. I *definitely* wasn't going to make it to that. Jason's rehearsal dinner…wasn't going to that either. I didn't even know what time of day it was or if it was even the same day I last remembered. I'd never been so lost and confused in my life. How odd it felt to have no control of anything, to not know what was going on or what was to happen next.

I wasn't sure how long I had been walking when I saw what appeared to be faint lights in the distance. I tilted my head and squinted my eyes to try to see better. What were they? Lights? Stars? They were scattered around in what looked to be no organized pattern. I picked up my pace to get closer to whatever this was.

I wasn't sure what I was going to find or what I was going to encounter, but at this point, did I really have a choice? Aside from the storage unit I woke up in, this was the only thing other than dirt that I'd encountered. As I got closer I realized the smoke in the air was moving. The lights got brighter, and the closer I got, I saw they were part of a building. A huge building as a matter of fact. It looked like a combination of a factory and a construction site of some sort. There were railings, stairs, gravel, and giant pipes that had smoke coming out of them. Talk about pollution.

It appeared to be abandoned but why were the lights on? And where was the smoke coming from? Ugh, more questions. The building was quite a few feet down on the bottom of the hill, closed off by a fence. I debated on whether I should go down and check it out or if I should keep walking and see what else I would run into.

"Hello?" I called out faintly. Okay, so my voice was still working. "HELLO?!" I shouted. I heard my voice echo out into the distance but didn't hear any type of response. I was alone. I sighed with frustration. Frustrated with the fact that here was this building that I had no connection to or even knew what it was, and the fact that I was completely alone. It was as if I were isolated from everything. Where is everyone? Even in Tijeras I was bound to see someone. But so far, not a bird in the sky nor a car passing by. Nothing.

One thing I did realize from this building was that there *were* other things out here. I just had to find them. I decided I would skip on checking out this place. If I had to, I would come back to it. All I had to do was turn around and follow the road back. Right?

I kept walking ahead with the image of the factory in my mind. The more I thought about it, the more I began to convince myself that I'd seen it before. Then I remembered the times my friends and I drove by Tijeras, that same factory was always visible on the other side of the highway. Of course, I never actually bothered to ask what it was—I just took note of its existence. It was just a building you passed on the side of the road. But that did mean one thing: I was getting closer to Albuquerque.

I know I was nowhere near where I wanted to be. I was a good ten or so miles from reaching the outskirts of Albuquerque. The visibility of it all was still an issue, because I was only assuming that I was going the right way. I didn't know for sure. Out of the thickness of the fog I began to see street lights. I thought I was hallucinating, but as I got closer I began to see stop signs, buildings, stoplights, street signs, trees, and even the road I was walking on turned into an actual black road with traffic dividers printed in the middle. But this couldn't be right. I turned around to where I just came from and tried to make sense of it. If the building I just passed was the one I was thinking about (and I was more than positive that it was) then I should still be on the highway. There should be nothing for miles to come. So, where was I?

As I looked around, I began to recognize the sights that surrounded me. Up ahead was the downtown movie theater off to the right was the Albuquerque Convention Center, several hotels in the distance, and the train station was to my left. I was in downtown Albuquerque.

But how? This was downtown—there was no doubt about it. But given the walking distance, it should've taken several hours to get here. I couldn't make sense of how I got here so fast but at least I was somewhere I knew. I kept walking down the street, looking all around, hoping to encounter something or someone. Where was everyone? It felt as if I was the only person left in the world. Strange, I've never seen this place so calm, so quiet. My footsteps made loud sounds as they touched the ground, something I never could hear when I was downtown.

Some buildings had lights on while others had the lights off. I looked through windows but they were empty. I tried to open a few doors to places as I passed but all of them were locked. Strange. I looked at the street I was on: Central and 3rd St. Now that I knew exactly where I was, I didn't feel as good as I hoped I would. On the contrary, I began to get worried. Why was I alone? Why wasn't there anybody around?

Just as I asked those questions, I noticed a figure in the distance standing with its back toward me. He or she was wearing a black hoodie and black sweats. I couldn't tell but it looked like they had a hat on. The image of my attacker flashed through my mind. Was this the same person?

Well, I got what I wanted but I wasn't happy about it. Who was this person? Were they safe? Did they have answers? Again, with the questions… I wondered if I should make myself noticed. The fact that they hadn't moved made me think that they hadn't noticed I was here. But didn't they hear my footsteps? I looked around to see if there was anyone else around and again found no one. I took a quiet step forward to try and get a better glimpse of this person. They appeared to be looking down at something. I tilted my head to try and see what but the fog was too thick.

A few beats passed and I decided to make myself known. "Hello?"

The figure shot its head up. They seemed to be taken completely by surprise that I was there. When they turned around I saw that the figure was a guy. I was right about the hat but his face held no recognition to me. I didn't believe I'd ever seen him before. I always had a skill for remembering faces rather than names. His face looked pale. He had sad looking blue eyes, shaven face with acne scars, black bangs peaked from under his hat, and he had a puzzled look on his face. Not sure what age I would put him under. Twenty-one? Twenty-two? More importantly, was he going to say something?

We just stared at each other for a few moments. He inspected me up and down and I concluded that he was just as lost as I was. He kept his hands in the pockets of his hoodie and didn't speak. He reminded me of one of those kids at schools that were always alone and withdrawn from everyone else.

"And you are?" he finally asked. His voice sounded so monotone, so bland, like it was missing character.

"Confused," I responded, "and you?"

He chuckled. "That's a pretty sad name"

So, he *did* have character—I stood corrected. A smartass remark, I noticed as well. Who was this guy and why was he here? I wasn't in the mood to throw smart remarks back and forth, but if that's how he wanted to play, let's go.

He responded again before I could answer. "My name is Axel."

I bit my tongue. I could stay a mystery or I could comply. So, Axel was his name. well, what was his story? Why was he here? I wanted answers. I had already given away that I was in a confused state, stupid move. He probably thought he had the upper hand.

"Where is everyone?" I asked.

"What," he countered, "not going to tell me your name?"

"You have your name, what do you need mine for?" I knew this wasn't the way I was going to get answers. I realized I was coming off as kind of a jerk, but hey, he started it.

He closed his eyes and chuckled again. "Whatever then. Do you think you could at least tell me *her* name?" He shifted his body and I saw what he had been looking down on. From this angle, I could make out a girl lying on the floor with body made out in a weird shape. I took a step closer to get a better view and he seemed to take a step back, keeping his distance. Was he scared of me?

"Chill," I assured him. He kept his guard up. Even when I looked away, I knew he was still looking at me. As I got closer to the girl, I got the unnerving feeling that she was dead. She had blonde hair, brown eyes, and had on an outfit that looked like she was going out for a fun time. She looked young, probably around my age. It was probably the red stilettos she was wearing, or the short red dress she had on, but either way she looked like a total babe. There was blood coming out the side of her mouth and her eyes were open but they weren't looking at anything, just staring.

I swallowed hard and turned to Axel. No surprise that he was still watching me closely. Still no answers to any of my questions. And now I had even more questions. Who was this chick? How did she die? So, I'd encountered two people since I'd woken up. One was an ass and one was dead. Both were less that useless to me at this point.

"Talk," I demanded as I pointed to the girl.

Axel raised an eyebrow and remained still. "Don't give me orders."

"You were the one that attacked me," I accused. "You attack her as well?" I didn't believe it was him that was in my house. But I had to shake him up somehow.

"What are you talking about?" he tried. "I just ran into her. A few moments later, *you* showed up. Maybe *you* killed her."

"Why is she dead?"

"I don't know."

"Where is everyone?"

"I don't *know*."

"What *do* you know?"

"That you need to lay off your questions." He was getting agitated and it was clear that my words were getting to him. No one ever liked being interrogated and this guy was no different. As frustrated as he was becoming, it was clear that he had no answers to any of the questions I had.

"Or what?" I challenged.

He seemed to be choosing his words carefully. After a few beats, he said "Look, I'm just trying to find my brother."

His words took me by surprise. His brother? So, there *were* other people here besides just us. Where was his brother then? Where did he come from? Why were they separated? He wasn't giving me a lot of information to go off of. Instead, he just gave me more questions to wonder about.

"We got…separated, and I would like to find him."

Was he asking me for help? Not directly anyways, but he did lay on a big hint that he had a task on hand. I was looking for things, too. Not specifics, but I was still looking as well. Not that I would disclose that to him.

"Sounds like a personal problem." I replied.

Axel didn't respond, he just stared at me. I felt like I wasn't going to get anything useful out of him so I started to turn away. I wasn't sure where I was going but I had to find something or someone else. Axel was clueless therefore he served as no use to me. I may have not approached him in the kindest of ways but that was how I always got what I wanted: by force. I still wanted to try and get more out of him but he had nothing more to offer so I didn't see any point to hanging around.

"Running away?" He teased.

"I'm actually walking," I called back. "In case you can't tell the difference between the two."

I didn't get very far before I heard him say "Wait."

I wanted him to ask me again. I always got fueled by the needs of others. I always had what others needed. Answers, money, stuff… I don't think I could offer Axel anything much besides company at this point, but something was better than nothing.

"Where did she go?" He asked. It took me a moment before I realized he had meant the chick on the floor. I stopped in my tracks and then turned around. He was right—she was no longer there. My eyes scanned the scene before me but she was nowhere in sight. I was more than sure she was dead, so she couldn't have just gotten up and walked away. And without making a sound nonetheless.

I opened my mouth to say something but decided against it. I looked up at Axel and he looked more frightened than he did confused. He just stared at me as if I knew where this girl had gone. Where was his bad boy act now? "I'm done here," I told him.

I turned back around and a scream got caught in my throat. I jumped back and dropped my jaw. The dead girl we had just seen on the floor was standing a few feet in front of me.

III

Undaunted

"How'd you do that?" asked Axel.

The chick looked taken back. "Do what?" She didn't have the "dead" aspect anymore. She looked rather very alive, and lost. Her face was no longer pale and the blood by her mouth was gone. Her blonde hair was now done in a half-up, half-down style, straight except for light curls passing her shoulders. She had a soft voice that had an innocent tone to it. I couldn't help but stare at her from head to toe. I could make out average-sized cleavage from her red halter dress covered by a dark denim jacket. I hadn't seen many rational things since I woke up, and this wasn't in that category either. So…she wasn't dead? But I had just seen her. Axel had seen her as well so I know I wasn't imagining it. She took note of my inspections.

"Can I help you?" she asked.

Okay, I knew I was being weird by staring but I couldn't help myself. I had so many questions I wanted to ask. Who are you? Are you dead? How did you get from the floor to here? Do you know what's going on? I opened my mouth but couldn't find my voice.

"Maybe you can help *me*," piped in Axel. I turned around to him, I felt a twinge of jealousy of the fact that he managed to get words out and I didn't. "I'm looking for my brother."

"She wasn't talking to *you*," I snarled.

"Maybe not," he said, "but I know where my voice is. You seemed to have a little trouble finding yours."

"No trouble at all," I spat.

He chuckled to himself. He was really starting to get under my skin. So, I didn't have the words to say anything. Could he blame me? She was just *dead*! Or maybe not. I needed to know. I had to recover my image. I just needed to ask the obvious and demand answers.

"Okay, look," I began, "I don't know what's going on. Ummm… Are you dead? Because you look very much alive right now."

She wasn't looking at either of us anymore. She was just staring out with a blank expression. Was she even listening to me? I never had patience when it came to not knowing things. How hard was it for her to answer my question?

I pushed it some more. "A simple 'yes' or 'no' would great."

Still no answer. Her facial expression looked like she was trying to decipher something complicated, it was no longer blank. What was she looking at? I looked back at Axel but he was waiting for an answer as well. With a sigh of frustration, I tried her once more. "*Hello?*"

"Lay off," warned Axel.

"No," I called back to him before trying her again. "Hey, are you even listening to me?"

She gasped with a shock. She looked alarmed like she seemed to have either remembered or just figured something out. She turned around to the building behind her and looked around it before stopping at the top. If my memory served me right, this was a hotel. Not sure which one. Downtown had many hotels. It was hard to keep up with their names. But it didn't really seem like it mattered at this point to anyone but her. I also took note of the bright red bow in the middle of her hair. Thick ribbon, too. Maybe three inches? Something the cheerleaders around school would be seen wearing.

"Oh, my god," she managed. She began gasping for air, her breathing sounded like she had just run a marathon. She ran her hands through her blonde hair and then began inspecting her body. Her eyes widened and she looked frightened. Did she just remember something? Can she be of some use now?

She turned back to me. "He did it," she whispered.

"He?" I replied. "He, who? Did what?"

"He really did it." It sounded like she was talking to herself more than she was to me. Who was she talking about? I don't think she was talking about Axel. Did that mean there was someone else here? And what did *he* do? UGH! Even *more* questions to think about.

"What's your name?" asked Axel.

"Screw names!" I yelled. "*What* is going on and *who* are you talking about?" All patience was gone. What did it matter what her name was? We had more important things to figure out, and these two were pointless.

"Why are you yelling?" asked Axel, "I just asked what her name was."

"Yes, I heard you." How can he be so calm about all this? Here we were in downtown Albuquerque, a place that had a population of over 900,000 people, and there were now only three. Well, five if you counted Axel's brother that I had yet to see and whoever "he" was that this chick was talking about. I was starting to freak out and it was becoming harder to maintain my image. "I don't think names are in any way helpful. Shouldn't you be wondering why there's no one else here? Why everything's abandoned? Or what we're even doing here in the first place?"

"Lennox," said the chick.

That was random. "*What?*"

"My name is Lennox."

"Nice to meet you," said Axel. "My name's Axel."

Were they seriously introducing themselves like this was some sort of casual encounter? "Congratulations." My sarcastic tone couldn't be more obvious. "Find each other on Facebook, take selfies, and post status updates on what a wonderful time you guys are having. If you'll excuse me, I have answers to find."

I turned around and began walking away. I wasn't about to introduce myself and start idle conversations with those two. I still wanted answers before I started to ask any more questions. I wasn't sure where I was going. I knew all of Albuquerque like the back of my hand but something was going on, something wasn't right. How did I manage to get all the way from Tijeras to Albuquerque in a matter of a few footsteps? Where was everything else in between? More questions were starting to get asked, and I was getting more frustrated.

"Wait, where are you going?" called back Lennox, again with that same calm tone that Axel had. She was just panicking about something a few minutes ago. Talk about bipolar.

"Don't worry about it."

"You don't know what's out there."

"It's Albuquerque, of course I do."

I heard her heels stepping toward me as well as Axel's footsteps. Of course, they would follow me. "That's not what I mean. Look around, you don't know what's going on, do you?"

"Oh, and I suppose you do?"

"As a matter of fact, yes."

I stopped short. *What?* Was she serious? How did she? I turned around to face them. "Bluff."

"It's not that hard to figure out. If you would drop your 'tough guy' act you would see things more clearly."

Was she lecturing me? The nerve of this girl. She didn't even know me. "And what *is* going on? According to you."

"Well," she began as she ran her hands down the side of her skirt, "to answer your question from earlier… Yes. I am dead."

What?! She's dead? How can that be? How was she so sure? And how could she talk about it so calmly? I had questioned it earlier when I saw her lying lifeless on the floor. but I didn't believe it now. She was alive.

Of course, she was. She was standing right in front of me looking alive and well. "And you know this how?"

"Because I remember everything that was happening right before my death."

I looked over to Axel. He had his arms crossed in front of his chest and was staring at the floor. "Are you buying this?" I asked him. He lifted his head and met my eyes but didn't say anything.

"Okay." I turned back to Lennox. "So you're dead. Then what are you? A ghost? Spirit?"

"Neither. I don't think I've fully crossed over yet."

I wasn't convinced. "Stop. Get off it. You're not dead."

"Of course, I am. There's no way I survived that." She looked back and up the building. Survived what?

"Well, you look just fine to me." She turned back to me as I continued, "Even if you were dead, which I assume that you're not 'cause you're clearly walking and talking like this is some light subject. How does that explain everything else?"

She gave a light chuckle. "You still don't get it, do you?"

"I get it," interjected Axel.

"Well good for you," I told him. "Are you going to tell me you're dead, too?"

Axel didn't say anything. None of their words were making sense. How was it that they both remembered things when I didn't? If Lennox really was dead, why would she be here of all places?

"What's your name?" she asked.

I didn't want to answer. But I did want to start answering all the questions I had. I bit down on my tongue for a few seconds before answering. "Zanniel."

"Well, Zanniel," she began, "since you can't seem to put it together on your own, I'll put it in the simplest way I can."

I raised my eyebrows as I waited for her to talk again.

"You're dead, too."

I paused as I tried to make sense of her words. I was dead? How? Why? She had no evidence of this. Just because she thought she was dead didn't mean we all were. Sure, there was something strange going on, but it was not death. After a few seconds, I couldn't hold it in any longer. My lips spread into a wide grin. I closed my eyes and began to laugh. A small chuckle at first, then I burst into hysterical laughter. She was kidding, right? Dead? Me? Ha!

"Quite the sense of humor you have," said Lennox. "Would you mind filling us in on the joke?"

It took me a little longer than I felt necessary to compose myself. After the moment passed, I could speak again. "You're the joke."

"Me?" She sounded surprised by my words.

"Wait, no, *both* of you."

"How am I a joke?" asked Axel sounding insulted.

"Do you seriously expect me to believe that there's any truth to what you're saying?"

Lennox narrowed her eyes at me. She looked offended but she maintained her position. "I don't expect you to believe anything. I'm simply telling you what I know. What you choose to do with that information is your business."

She wants to keep up this charade? Fine. "Okay. Tell me then, how did I die?"

She opened her mouth to say something but decided against it. She swallowed hard and crossed her arms. "I don't know."

"No? Okay. So, if you don't know *how* I died, then how do you know I *am*?"

She was starting to lose her patience; the frustration was starting to be noticeable on her face. "Because of where we are."

"Oh really? And where are we exactly? Last I checked, we were in Albuquerque."

"I think…we're in Limbo."

Limbo? Where was she getting all this? How confident was she about the things she was saying? I could shake her up a little more. "Oh, you *think*? So, you're not even *positive* that that's where we are?"

She didn't answer, she just stared at me with a pained expression. "Answer me this, *Lennox*, if in fact we are in this supposed Limbo of yours, why is it that it looks just like downtown?"

She closed her eyes. "I don't know."

"Why are we the only ones here?"

"I-don't-know."

"Really? How do you not know all of this if just a few seconds ago you were so sure of yourself?"

"She was just trying to help," said Axel, "no need to act like such a dick."

"I'm no actor."

Axel gave a scoff and turned away. I turned back to Lennox. "Here's what *I* know: I may be a little lost and confused, but I'm not dead. Just because you think you are doesn't mean I am. I—"

I couldn't finish my sentence. Something from behind Lennox caught my eye. Someone else was here. I couldn't see much from the fog that was around us, but I know I saw someone. I walked over to get a closer look. As I did, the figure seemed to move away and began to run. I started to run, too. From a few feet in front of me I could make out a person running away from me at full speed. Why were they running? Who was this person?

"Hey!" I yelled, but got no response. I chased them all the way passed to movie theater from the way I'd come. They seemed to have taken off to the path that would take me back to Tijeras. I slowed my running as I tried to make sense of it. The figure kept running. From behind, I heard Lennox and Axel coming toward me. Did they see the figure, too?

"What are you doing?" asked Lennox as they eventually caught up to me.

"I saw someone," I replied.

28

"So, you chase them?"

I turned to her. "Why are you following me?"

"Look, you may not choose to accept what's going on. But why not give me a chance to explain everything that I *do* know and then you can decide if I'm right or not."

"Not interested." I know how stubborn I am with my ways. I always won arguments that I knew I was completely wrong in. The way I always saw it, if I can convince myself I was right at something, then I could convince someone else. But as not interested as I wanted to be, I didn't convince myself. I *did* want to know what Lennox knew. If I really was dead, then it would take a lot of convincing on her part. "…but willing."

IV

Encounters

I HATED THE FEELING OF not knowing. I always had to be in the loop of things, in on the joke, or simply informed about anything and everything. When I wasn't, I wouldn't stop until I found out everything I needed to know. That's why I chose journalism as a career; I was great at uncovering things. With that said, who had I just seen? I'm guessing that they had seen me as well. But why would they run from me? Did they know me? Part of me did believe in the nonsense that Lennox was speaking about. I had been attacked after all, and that was the last memory I had prior to waking up here. I wasn't about to disclose that information to either her or Axel. The less they knew about me the better.

"Tell me," I started, "why do you think we're all dead?" I kept a steady pace as I walked in the lead with both of them close behind. I wasn't sure where exactly we were headed but whoever it was that I'd seen was heading this way. If Lennox was going to convince me that I was dead, she really needed to try and she needed to try hard, 'cause at this point, I was only talking about death to entertain the thought, not that I really believed any of it.

"Because it makes sense. Didn't you ever go to Sunday Mass? Or even think or talk about what happens after you die?"

"No." I was Catholic by my parent's decision but I never practiced it. I stopped going to church ever since I was a kid. I got baptized, but that's as far I got. I never did my first Holy Communion, my confirmation, or even went to confession. "You're telling me this has to do with religion?"

"Well, of course," she replied. "When someone dies, they either go to heaven or to hell; depending on the choices they've made. However, there's also the in-between, like I said before, Limbo."

"Meaning?"

"Meaning that they haven't fully crossed over. A last judgement, if you would. They're not innocent nor are they completely malicious. They have as much good in them as they do bad."

"You mean like purgatory?" asked Axel.

"In a way, yes," she answered. "If I had to guess—"

"Guessing gets you nowhere," I interrupted. "It just means you don't fully know what it is you're talking about. You can guess about something all day and night but in the end if you don't know for sure, then you know nothing."

"If I had to guess," she said again with a slight irritated tone, "I would say we all have done things in life that we're not so proud of. We haven't crossed over because our fates have yet to be determined."

This was her way of convincing me? "Enough with all the religious bullshit, Lennox. That still doesn't explain how you know we're dead."

"Because it all makes sense!"

How?! I was getting frustrated. How can she tell me that all of this makes any sense? To her maybe, but that meant nothing if it was not clear to me. I knew what Limbo was, but how could she be so sure that that was where we were? One thing did stand out above the rest. "Let me try to make sense of it—what exactly did *you* do that you're not so proud of?"

Her silence gave her shame away. She didn't answer right away which made me believe there was more to this chick than what meets the eye. "Things. I wouldn't know where to begin. Well, I do actually. But it's rather a long story."

She spoke in a low voice that made me want more. "I think I've got time—talk."

"What about *you?*" asked Axel. His question caught me off guard.

"What *about* me?" I was playing dumb. I knew exactly what he was getting at. But I found it fun having others waste their breath and words explaining things I already knew.

"What did you do to put yourself in this situation?"

Exactly what I thought he meant. What was it to him? Or even to Lennox? They didn't know me, nor did they need to. Of course, they wanted to know more about me. Who didn't? I loved having the upper hand, though. We could all sit around and explain about all the horrible things we did in life. But what was the fun in that? All that would do is give off the impression that I actually gave a shit about them.

I gave a light chuckle. "Don't worry about it."

We kept walking until we came up to the strange factory I had seen earlier. Through the thick fog, I could start to make out the lights, the railings, and everything I had seen earlier. "If this is the best you got, Lennox, I'm not convinced."

As I stared at the building before me, everything looked the same except there were cars here now. Cars that weren't here the first time I passed by. Off the cliff was a broken beaten black car on its side. As I looked closer to the factory, there was a white police car with its lights faintly flashing red and blue. In front of it, a red car was parked with the driver door wide open. The trashed car looked like it had gotten into a bad accident and the other car looked to have just been pulled over. What happened?

Before Lennox could reply to my comment, Axel began shrieking out of nowhere. "Benny!"

Benny? He continued to shout the name as he took off running downhill toward the beaten car. Was Benny this so-called brother he was looking for? Did he see him? I turned to Lennox and she looked just as shocked as I was.

I made my way down the cliff to catch up with Axel. Lennox followed behind. How could she walk in those heels? They had to be at least five inches high. But without a slip or a trip, we both made it down and caught up to him. He was breathing heavily. Not because he was out of breath but because he seemed scared, almost panicked. He reminded me of the way Lennox was acting the first time we encountered her.

Axel searched the car all around repeatedly. What was he expecting to find? "I don't think there's anyone in there," I pointed out the obvious.

"Benny…" he continued, "no, no, no…" His voice had that nervous tone to it, the kind you get when you sound like you're about to start crying.

"Who's Benny?" asked Lennox.

"My *brother*," he snapped.

"Did…you see him just now?"

"No."

"Then what makes you think he's here?"

"Because he *was*!" Lennox kept trying to approach Axel in a calm way but he wasn't having it; he looked he was getting frustrated. He was so sure that his brother was here. I looked around to see if I saw sign of anyone else, but there was no one. Not until I looked up toward the factory. There, on the second floor stood a figure that I could only make out from the fog to be wearing the same mask my attacker was. I blinked a few times to make sure I wasn't imagining it. I even shut my eyes and shook my head. When I opened them, the figure was still there.

My body acted before my mind could make sense of it. Before I knew it, I took off to the building and began climbing the stairs. I took them two at a time, racing to top. I had to see who this was. I heard Lennox call after me, but paid no attention. When I got up to the spot I had seen the figure standing, no one was here. The only thing here was the mask I had seen. It was placed on the floor as if whoever left it here wanted me to find it. What did this mean? Who else was here?

I picked up the mask and held it up to my face. As I inspected it, there were spots on the white mask that appeared to be dry blood. Was that…my blood? And what was with the duct tape over the mouth in the shape of an X? I looked over the railings down to Lennox and Axel by the car. If Lennox was so sure she was dead, then that meant she knew how she died. I didn't want to accept the fact that I was dead, but I began to believe that Lennox was right. Only how? I don't remember dying. All I remember was lying on the floor of my house looking into the eyes of this mask as everything went black. Was that death? Did I die then and there?

Then I thought of Axel and realized something. New wonders and questions began popping up in my head as I began to head back down to them. If Axel had said he got what Lennox was talking about earlier, then that meant he thought he was dead, too. He was looking for his brother, which could only mean they'd died together, but why wasn't his brother anywhere around? Could it be what Lennox was saying about us not fully crossing over yet? I felt stupid for actually buying the things she had told me. It sounded so childish and made up.

As I reached the bottom of the stairs and started heading back, I heard a noise and whipped my head around. It sounded like poles hitting each other, but when I looked back, there was nothing. I turned around and found two hands closing their grip on my neck. My first thought was to scream but I couldn't. I tried to gasp for air but my body didn't need it. The person in front of me had their hood pulled over head. All I could see were teeth clenched together in a snarl. I let go of the mask and tried to free myself from their grasp.

I'd never been choked before, but I would assume a person would begin to feel light headed or begin to black out. However, that wasn't case. I found myself not fighting for life but simply fighting to get free. Before I knew it, I was let go. I was on my hands and knees trying to comprehend what had just happened. Whoever was choking me, was being pulled away by someone else. They were kicking and struggling but the other person was clearly stronger. I saw Lennox running toward me. What use was she now? I was just being choked and she was nowhere to offer me any kind of help when I needed it. Useless, both her and Axel.

"Enough!" demanded one of the figures. When I got a better view, it was a cop. Probably the owner of the police car parked out front. He looked young, too. Probably in his early twenties. Dressed in his black uniform, he had blue eyes, blond buzz cut, and he had a body that looked like he drank one too many protein shakes. That, or he was a part-time body builder. Either way, he was swollen.

He appeared to be bigger than the hooded figure he'd pulled off me. As he continued to struggle, his hood fell back and I got a clear view of his face. A face I had seen not that long ago. A face I *knew*. His black bangs fell over his forehead, and his angry black eyes looked back at me. His skin whiter than a ghost, yet unmistakable. "Satchel?"

I said his name as if I were asking, but I wasn't. I knew exactly who he was. Why him of all people? Why was he *attacking* me just now? In a way, I was happy to see a familiar face but I wasn't happy to see *him*. Why was he here?

"Ah said *ENOUGH*!" yelled the cop. Satchel kept fighting to break loose from his restraint, but the cop was just too big. He could probably snap Satchel in half if he wanted to.

Satchel seemed determined. "Get off me!"

"You know him?" I looked up to see Lennox come closer to see what was going on. Axel was still back at the beat-up car. What did it matter to her if we knew each other or not? I got up to my feet to try to compose myself.

I ignored Lennox completely. "Why are you here?" I turned my attention to Satchel. What was his problem? He seemed like a completely different person than when I had seen him at UNM not too long ago. It seemed like it happened just yesterday. At least that was what it felt like. I was completely unaware of what day or even what time it was. The fog didn't help me see the sky, and no one really seemed to know what was going on. Like usual, I had to figure things out on my own.

"Same reason you are," managed Satchel. The cop still had a firm grip on him and didn't look like he was going to let go anytime soon. Same reason *I* was? What did *that* mean?

I had to be bold, show no fear. "Stalker much? First you wait by my car and then you show up here? What's this new obsession you have with me?" Nothing made sense even before I woke up here. Satchel had been gone for over a year and he randomly shows up the day that I'm supposed to leave for Kentucky? And now I find him here of all places.

"Don't flatter yourself," he replied. "Not everything's about you, Zephyr. Not anymore."

"Okay. So, what *is* this about, *man purse?*"

He barked a laugh. "What an ego you have. Don't tell me you don't remember what happened?"

Shit, he got me there; I really didn't have any idea what he was talking about. I tried to keep a straight face to show that I knew everything, but there was a long pause that more than likely gave me away. I stared at him for a few more beats. I had to keep him talking. Maybe I would figure something out on my own. "With? I'm a busy guy. I don't keep up with everything going on around me."

He closed his eyes and giggled a little. By this point I think he found it pointless to try and escape the cop's grasp. He stopped fighting back. "When are you going to open your eyes and see things for what they really are?"

It sounded like he said it as more of a statement rather than to me directly. Open my eyes to what? Ugh! I'm over this nonsense. I didn't need to waste any more time here. I had questions and I needed answers. "Don't come at me with pointless phrases. If you have nothing productive to say, better not say anything at all."

"Can someone please clue me in?" asked Lennox. "Who are you exactly?"

Her eyes darted from Satchel to the cop a few times. "Both of you," she clarified.

"Well," started the cop, "If this one 'ere can keep 'is hands to 'imself, we might be able to talk 'bout few things an' try to sort this out."

His tone of voice reminded me of that of a country boy. Not heavy on an accent, but you could tell he did have that appeal going for him. Not very intimidating either, like other cops tried to be. He didn't sound or even look that old either. He looked at Satchel for a few seconds, waiting for his response. Satchel couldn't look more agitated. "I'm cool," he assured.

Once the cop let go, Satchel yanked his arms free and turned around to face him. His facial expression changed from being mad to being bothered once he saw who was restraining him. "Oh," he complained. "It's *you*."

It's *you*? *You* as in a cop or *you* as in a prior acquaintance? I wanted to ask but decided against it. Did Satchel know this cop? How? I thought it best to let them talk and see what I could pick up. Satchel looked around to Lennox. "And who the hell are *you*?"

Okay, so he knew of the cop, maybe, but not of Lennox and probably not Axel either. He must be as much of a stranger to them as I was. I couldn't handle staying quiet, I just couldn't. I always got what I wanted by looking for answers. But I couldn't just ask, I had to demand information. Before I could speak, Lennox answered.

"Excuse me," she replied, "I don't believe your tone is necessary." She was clearly offended by being approached in a harsh way. Whatever. It's what she gets for being so nosy. Satchel didn't respond, he just gawked at her.

Lennox took a deep breath. "Okay," she breathed, "Let's try this again. My name is Lennox and you obviously seem to know Zanniel already. His name is Axel—" she gestured toward him "—and who might you be?"

Satchel scoffed. "Not lookin' to make friends."

"That makes two of us," I agreed. It was getting irritating having to hear Lennox talk to everyone like this was some sort of normal occasion. "So, talk. Why are you here?"

"I already told you."

"Yeah," I countered, "and what was *that* supposed to mean?"

He rolled his eyes. "Come on, Zephyr, you're smarter than that."

Ugh! I hated being called by my last name. I always saw that as a sign of disrespect toward me. Or even having nicknames given to me without my approval was equally annoying. Names like Double Z, Zan', or even Zanny. My name was Zanniel and I was to be addressed as such.

"Zephyr?" asked Lennox.

I rolled my eyes at her. "It's my *last* name, Lennox. Keep up."

"Yeah," continued Satchel, "quite the misnomer *that* is."

"Piss off, Satchel," I demanded, "you talk but you don't say anything. If you have nothing useful to say then just keep quiet."

Satchel threw me a smirk. He could tell he was getting under my skin and I unfortunately was giving the upper hand and satisfaction. He didn't blink. He held my gaze with intensity in his black eyes before speaking. "Why don't you make me?"

Was he seriously challenging me? "Maybe I will!"

I was not going to tolerate his nonsense. Nothing was making sense and Satchel wasn't helping the situation. If he wanted to throw down, then so be it. I'd been in a few fist fights that always ended with me as the victor. I wasn't afraid to get my point across by using physical matters. I stepped toward him and stopped when he spoke again.

"I killed you once already, Zephyr. I'd *love* to do it again."

V

Crossed

I ALWAYS KNEW PEOPLE ENVIED me. Those I knew and those I didn't. I never asked for success, popularity, talents, good looks, or anything of the type. Good things just seemed to come my way. Chicks wanted to be with me and guys wanted to *be* me. I lost track of who my real friends were after my freshmen year at the university, except for Tristan. All the other guys I befriended in high school seemed to go their own ways. It's not like it really mattered, I was going to be leaving this boring city and everything that inhabited it.

I could take the envy, the jealousy, and even the obsessions. But for someone to want me dead? That was an extreme that never even crossed my mind. I knew I did a few things here and there that I was not so proud of. But hearing Satchel tell me that he'd *killed* me turned Lennox's theory into a fact.

"What?" I asked, even though I had heard him clearly. His words seemed to echo in my ears. I stared at Satchel with disbelief. He killed me? He actually *killed* me? Why? How?

"D'you jus' confess to a murder?" asked the cop. His blue eyes darted from me to Satchel. The way his brow furrowed made me wonder what exactly he knew about this place. Was he dead, too? How could he ask Satchel if he'd committed murder when his victim was standing in front of him looking perfectly fine? I quickly thought back to what Lennox had said about her being dead. Did that mean the cop and Satchel were dead? Were we *all* dead?

Satchel turned to the cop. "Sorry, officer. I have the right to remain silent." The sarcasm in his tone was obvious. The cop, however, did not look amused.

"Sure ya do," he said.

We all turned our attention back to Axel when he gave a loud and angry grunt. I forgot he was still back at the car. For a moment, I had forgotten that he was here at all. He was hunched over the car like he was protecting it in some way. What was his deal? He yelled out "Benny!" once again, which got Lennox walking toward him. She looked back over her shoulder once before heading to him.

I turned my attention back to Satchel. "You killed me?"

I knew how pathetic I sounded, but I wasn't really trying to protect my image at this point. All I really wanted now were answers. Was that too much to ask? Satchel seemed like he knew everything that was going on around him like Axel and Lennox did. But, why didn't *I*? I wonder if the cop knew what was going on as well.

Satchel chuckled at my question. "Can I do it again?" I glared back at him trying to process his words. According to what he was saying, he not only killed me but he seemed to be proud of it. Almost like he was bragging. But as I stared back I couldn't escape the thought that if I was dead, he must be too. He had to be. Why else would he be here? I'm not sure exactly what emotion I was feeling. Anger? Disgust? Fear? I was in a blank state. I no longer had an urge to fight. All I really wanted was an explanation.

"How did you—why?"

"'kay," interrupted the cop, "how's 'bout we join them two over there an' we can talk more of this as a group." Was he seriously giving us orders? I don't believe he had any sense of authority here. I wanted to say a smart remark but I bit my tongue instead. I turned back to Satchel and waited for him to move first.

The cop seemed to sense the tension that was still in the air. "Cut yer crap, the two a' ya."

He gave Satchel a slight shove on the shoulder but he didn't take that too kindly. "Don't touch me!" I wondered if Satchel could feel? I hadn't been able to ask the others if they could physically feel things without sounding weak or lost. So, I'd refrained.

"Then *go*," he demanded. Satchel had turned toward the cop as if he was about to fight. Satchel was nowhere near the size the cop was. He turned to me once then headed toward the others. I didn't wait to be told twice. So, I started walking after Satchel did. I always had a problem with authority figures. Not that I paid them no respect but I always felt like they abused their power. They made it seem like just 'cause they could, they would treat others as they wanted. Cops especially.

Once we reached them, Axel had his fists and his forehead pressed on the car. He was mumbling something to himself but I couldn't make out what he was saying. His eyes were closed shut and he seemed to be shaking. I looked over to Lennox who had her arms crossed over her chest and was staring at him.

"What's *his* deal?" I asked. Lennox looked to me and shrugged her shoulders. I looked around the car a little more carefully. There were pieces of glass scattered all over the ground that seemed to go up until the hill started. Engine oil, gas, or some other car fluid was also all over the place. Seeing the car on its side and looking at the mess before me brought me to believe that it came crashing down from the top of the hill.

"Axel?" asked Lennox. She gently placed her hand on his back and seemed to be choosing her words carefully. "...Were you in there when this happened?" Axel didn't move or respond. Was this how he died? In some sort of car accident? I had to hand it to Lennox, she had a soft and gentle way of approaching things. The exact opposite of how I would've handled it. Maybe I should let her do the talking, let's see if she can get more out of Axel than I did.

"You have no obligation to talk about it if you don't want to," she continued, "but I have a hunch that this was where you passed. And if my hunch is correct, your brother Benny passed with you as well, didn't he?"

She was on to something. *Of course* this is how he died! I had seen that one coming. If Lennox's hunch was correct, where was Benny in all of this? Had he been the one that had run from me earlier? Or had it been Satchel or even the cop?

Lennox continued talking. "Only your brother isn't here. Do you think he might have survived?"

Axel's head shot up and he met his eyes to Lennox's before looking around to everyone else. His face was red and his eyes were starting to gather tears. Lennox waited for Axel to respond before continuing.

Axel's bottom lip started to tremble. "No," he said in a high pitch, "he didn't!" He was definitely on the verge of crying, it was obvious. How was he so sure he was dead? I wanted to ask so badly but Axel seemed to be more open to talking to Lennox than he was to me. Axel's eyes were open but he didn't seem to be looking at anything in particular; he just stared. Tears began to fall on the sides of his cheeks. His bottom lip continued to tremble as he began to sob. He backed away from the car and removed his hat. As he fell to his knees, he put his face in his hat with both hands pressed up and began crying into it. He officially broke down.

"I'm sorry!" he cried. "I'm so sorry!"

Lennox's jaw dropped. She looked around to and the others for support, but we were all just as surprised as she was. What was he sorry for? Why the sudden melt down? I looked over to Satchel and the cop. They were just staring down at Axel. I wanted to get more information from Satchel about my death, but I didn't feel like this was the right time to do so.

Lennox flipped her blonde hair back and took a deep breath. She got Axel started, she might as well make him finish. She squatted down next to him and began rubbing his back, though I doubted that he could feel her. Moral support seemed like the only thing she could offer.

"Hey…" she whispered to him.

Axel's sobs grew louder. I could never handle crying. If I ever felt the need to, I would always do it in private. Or, if I saw someone do it in public, I would assume they were just doing it for attention. I never saw the point of making others feel your pain or misery. However, I wasn't sure what to think of Axel crying. I wanted to make him explain. I wanted him to tell us what happened already. Well, it was obvious what happened. But, I wanted to know *how* he got there.

"Axel," pushed Lennox, "can you tell me what happened?"

"I didn't me-me-mean to," he sobbed. "I was just trying to be there for him! I-I-I didn't mean to—I'm sorry!"

It was hard to make out what he was trying to say. Lennox kept trying. "It's okay, sweetie. Shhh… Tell me what you remember."

He looked up at us. Either he was sweating, or he was crying an insane amount. His bangs were soaked, his face was completely red and wet. "He didn't do-o anything," he tried. "It shouldn't have ha-a-appened."

Lennox looked deep in thought. She wasn't getting much information to go from. She tried a different approach. "Okay, let's do this: tell me about your brother. Tell me about Benny. Can you try that?"

Axel took deep breaths as he tried to compose himself. After a few long beats, he found his voice again. He looked down at the floor as he spoke. "Benny wa-as my little brother," he began. "He looked u-up to me. I was his hero. When Benny was born, our parents split up. M-my mom took off and left us wi-ith our dad. I was only ten but I promised myself that I-I would always be there for Benny.

"And I was. Benny got sick when he-e was little. The doctors found tumors in his head and said he wouldn't live pa-past five. But he did. After Benny lived passed wha-at the doctors said, my dad stopped taking him back. He said the-ey were full of shit and didn't know what they were talking about. Said there was nothing wrong with him. Few months a-after that, our dad changed."

At least he could talk now with some occasional sniffles. So, he was a big brother. Good for him. Being an only child, I never knew what that must have been like. But that still didn't tell me anything about his death. Lennox was doing good on getting him to talk, but it hadn't answered any of the questions I had.

"How did your father change?" she asked.

"He just did. He stopped ca-aring about us. He was never at home anymore. Didn't care if we went to-to school or if we even ate. I got a job my sophomore year and a second job after I graduated. I wanted to go to co-ollege but I couldn't. Benny needed me to be there for him. I took on the pa-arent role. Got him clothes, food, took him to school and anything e-else he needed.

Lennox smiled at him. "I can see why Benny saw you as a hero."

A smile began to spread across Axel's face. "Yeah… Benny was amazing. Always did good in school… He had big dreams for being only nine. He wanted to be famous. He wanted to-o to make online videos, have subscribers… He was so i-innocent."

Up until this moment, I realized that I didn't know anything about Axel. All he was to me was a stranger that happened to be in the same place as me. I glanced at Lennox and the others and began to wonder about their back stories. I was hooked now. I found myself wanting to know things about this group. I felt like I would receive details in due time, but Axel wasn't done talking and Lennox wasn't done fishing for information.

"He was," she agreed. "What about you? What would you like us to know about you?"

"Well," he began, "not much about me, really. I'm nineteen years old. Worked at family-owned pizza joint and at a coffee shop downtown. I had no time for college 'cause I was always working. It got hard, you know? I didn't care that all I did wa-as work, but I got tired. After my night shifts were done, I would get home and have a drink from whatever liquor my dad left in the house. Not a lot, just some to relax. Benny didn't like it when I drank, so I would wait till he was a-asleep to do so."

That's it? What a boring life to live. How frustrating it must've been to do the same thing over and over again without progressing in life. Okay, he was doing it for his brother, I get that. But why didn't he reach out for help? He could've contacted some officials and explained his situation and have a load taken off his shoulders. If I were in his shoes, I would've done things differently. Of course, I kept those comments to myself for now. I did, however, bluntly ask, "So how did you die?"

Lennox shot me a disapproving look. I gave her a mocking look back. Could she blame me? I appreciate her efforts on getting him to talk but I wanted to speed things up a little. We already covered his basic life, didn't we? No sense wasting time on the small details.

"What Zanniel means," she comforted, "is how did your accident come to be?"

He thought to himself for a moment. "Our last night alive…

"Well… I came home after work. My dad wasn't there and Benny was already asleep. I thought my day was done so I grabbed a bottle and started drinking. I didn't know that I had crashed out but Benny woke me up saying he was hungry. It wasn't even late but I could feel my buzz from the alcohol kicking in and I couldn't tell Benny *no*. He had to eat, you know?

"I knew I shouldn't have been driving while I had alcohol in me but being the big brother that I was, I had to get Benny food. I didn't want Benny to come with me but he insisted. I was doing okay, I guess. We drove to a fast food place and we were on our way back. But…"

He was starting trail off. He squinted his eyes, trying to recall the events. "… I got lost, I guess. I took a wrong turn somewhere and we somehow ended up on the interstate leaving Albuquerque. Benny was getting concerned that it was taking longer than usual to get home and I kept assuring him that we were on our way.

"While I was driving, there was a car behind us. He was honking and flashing his lights and I guess he was in a hurry. I was doing good driving. I wasn't speeding. I was swerving a little but I was doing good. That car was on my ass and I didn't know why he didn't just pass me. Benny was getting scared and so was I. After he flashed his lights a few more times, I got blinded. He bumped the back of my car and passed us but…I lost control. All I could see was the bright flash in my eyes. Before I knew it, we had driven off the road and fell off the side of the cliff.

"I don't know how, but when I woke up I was on my side. I still had my seat belt on and everything was dark. I tasted blood in my mouth, couldn't feel my legs, and I smelled smoke. My windshield was smashed and I knew that I was in a wreck. I looked to my right and…and…"

Axel began to sob again. His breathing picked up a fast pace and his words seemed to come out in a rush. "… And I saw Benny and-and he wasn't moving. His eyes were staring back at me. I called his name but he wasn't answering me! I shook his shoulder but he wasn't responding! He had blood on the side of his face and on his-his-his mouth!"

He shut his eyes and broke down once more. He put his face in his hands and began bawling again. I looked over to the car and replayed everything he just said in my head. I was at a loss for words. That sounds like a shitty situation to be in. But where was Benny?

"My little brother!" he screamed, "Benny!"

He began to cry harder. "I'm sorry! I'm sorry, I'm sorry, I'm sorry!"

Lennox covered her mouth with her hand as tears fell on the sides of her face. The cop looked down at Axel with raised eyebrows and a fixed expression. Satchel's eyes were wide and his mouth hung open. He looked more shocked than the others.

"Axel," tried Lennox, "Axel, listen."

She reached out to touch his shoulder but he moved out of the way. He didn't look like he wanted to be comforted but Lennox kept trying. "No, you need to listen me, Axel. Benny knows you were only trying to be a good brother. You can't blame yourself for what happened. Things were out of your control, and you had no way of knowing about the events that were to occur."

It didn't seem like Lennox's words were getting through to him. Axel kept whispering "I'm sorry" through his sobs.

"I know," she said, "I know."

Satchel shifted his weight. He looked uncomfortable. He looked over to me, then back at Axel before speaking. "Hey, ummm…Axel?"

Axel looked up. He seemed to be surprised to be spoken to directly for the first time by Satchel. "I…" Satchel swallowed. He hesitated to talk. What words of comfort could Satchel possibly provide to make him feel better? He was a mess. Even I couldn't think of anything to say, which was odd because I always had something to say for everything. Still, I stared at him with curious eyes.

"I…" he tried again. All eyes were on him now. He looked at each one of us carefully before finally getting his words out. "I am…so sorry, Axel. That you went through all that. But, listening to your story and seeing *that* car right now. I'm pretty sure that the driver that ran you off the road was me."

VI

Exalted

ALL EYES WERE ON SATCHEL. So, he'd ended my life *and* Axel's? Not to mention his brother Benny's, as well. Talk about plot twist. Hearing Satchel say that he was the one who drove him off the road made Axel's story seem like it wasn't entirely his fault. Granted, Axel was under the influence while behind the wheel and that *did* play a major part in his death, but having Satchel being the one to initially cause the accident made it more his fault than anyone's. My main question was: why? Why did Satchel drive him off? I felt like if I waited a few moments, I was to find the answer.

Axel's eyes narrowed in on Satchel. "How?" He shook his head. "Wait, what? I don't even know you. What are you talking about?"

Satchel looked pained. "Look, it sounds crazy, I know, but answer me this: were you or were you not on this highway when you died?" He pointed up to the road we were on before. All our heads turned to where he gestured.

"I…" tried Axel.

"And were you or were you not in that car?" He then pointed to the beaten black car. Axel didn't reply. He just stared at Satchel with a blank expression, looking like he was trying to process what had just been said. Listening to Satchel, I began to get the familiar feeling I did when I woke up that everyone knew what was going on except me. Axel had an unfortunate but good memory of things. Lennox seemed to be familiar with the events going on but had yet to explain her death. The cop was still a mystery. And Satchel seemed to know more about my death than I did.

I wanted to know more. I wanted to know how this group of people died. Better yet, playing along with Lennox's theory, I wanted to know what everyone did that had kept them from fully crossing over. Listening to Axel tell his story, I was more than positive his contribution to his brothers' death was what has put him here.

"Okay," said Satchel, "Stop staring at me. Before any of you begin to put blame on anyone, I—"

Axel made Satchel cut his sentence short. Out of nowhere, he quickly got up and threw himself on Satchel, knocking him to the ground. Rage was written all over his face as he began thrashing his fists at Satchel's face. Thinking back to when I was being chocked, I doubted his punches were doing any real damage. Still, I felt a slight sense of contentedness seeing Satchel being beaten.

"THIS-IS-ALL-YOUR-FAULT!!!" shouted Axel with every blow being delivered. I looked over to Lennox, who was studying the sudden turn of events. She crossed her arms and tilted her head to the side. I was waiting for her to say something to them like *stop fighting*, or *violence doesn't solve anything* or something along those lines. But instead, she just stared quietly. The cop made his way over to the brawl and pulled Axel off. Darn, show's over.

Axel kept swinging. "Put me down!"

"Steady now," said the cop. "Yer' okay. It's done." He lifted Axel off with no struggle. He restrained his hands to keep from swinging and placed them behind his back to keep him still.

"Okay, wait," began Lennox, "how can you be so sure that the other driver was you?" Of course, Lennox couldn't stay quiet for too long. I rolled my eyes at her.

Satchel sat up. "I…" He looked at the ground and sighed. "I just know."

"Wow, Satchel," I teased. "Road rage much?"

"Piss off," he spat, still looking down, avoiding everyone's eyes. He must be feeling guilty. He had to be. He killed two innocent people, including me, and just told one of them about it. Talk about shameless. I could tell he was in a tough situation. I decided to push him further.

"Clear something up for us, would you?" I started pacing slowly. "So you say you killed me… *And* you ran Axel here off the road, causing him to lose control of his vehicle, initiating his fatal crash, which not only claimed his life but his little brother's as well?"

"We all heard 'im," said the cop. "No need to tell us again."

Where did *that* come from? Who was this guy anyway? Maybe my remarks were a little uncalled for, but that didn't mean he had to make note of them. I looked at him with glaring eyes. "And who might you be, officer?"

His eyes scanned the others before speaking. "Name's Clyde. Clyde Miller."

"Okay, Clyde, no one asked your input. So, don't give it." I know I may seem like I come off as rude with no manners—that's not it though. I say things the way I do to prove a point and to let others know where I stand.

Clyde smirked at me. "Some mouth ya got there, boy. Not sure who ya *think* ya might be, but ah hate to break it to ya, ya ain't more than any other person here." *What?* Was this guy trying to give me a lecture? Not sure who was more annoying at this point, him or Lennox.

I dismissed his words when I heard Satchel trying to talk again. "Axel, look, I am deeply sorry for the mess I caused you." Wasn't it a little late for apologies? I mean, the damage done was far beyond repair. But Satchel kept talking. "I'm not asking you to forgive me. I just need you to understand—"

"Save it," I interrupted. "You've done enough, don't you think?"

Satchel paid me no attention. "You have every right to hate me. The love you had for your brother, for Benny, I know the feeling."

I looked over to Axel now that Clyde let him go. He was no longer struggling now that Satchel had started talking. Axel was hanging on to every word that Satchel was saying and I got a feeling that I knew where he was going with his words.

"I too had a brother," Satchel continued, "and he was taken away from me by the actions of another." I knew it! I knew he was going to bring Fletcher up. Of course, he was trying to turn the tables so that this group would hate me just as much as he apparently did.

Axel picked his hat up off the ground and placed it back on his head. He still looked angry but he addressed Satchel in a calm tone. "You… you had a brother?"

"Yeah," agreed Satchel, "I *did*." No surprise he would try to find common ground with Axel seeing how vulnerable he was.

"What happened?" asked Axel. So that was it? Where was all the rage he was unleashing? He's looking into the eyes both his and his brother's killer and he wants to know how Satchel's brother died? Wow. Dying must not have affected him that bad if he was already making side conversation and getting to know his killer.

"Tell him, Zephyr." Satchel was looking at Axel but he was talking to me. Everyone else turned to face me now. I stood up straight and kept a composed face.

"There's nothing to tell," I said coolly.

Satchel scoffed. "Pathetic."

"Hold up," piped in Lennox. "You lost me again. You haven't told us how you know that *you* were the other driver. I don't see how Zanniel is relevant in this."

Satchel turned to Lennox. "Do you remember what happened right before you died?"

Lennox flinched, clearly caught off guard by the sudden question. "Of course I do."

"Okay then. So do I, and apparently so does Axel here." He turned to Clyde. "And you, *officer*?"

Clyde waited a few beats before answering. "Parts."

"Good," continued Satchel. "Some is better than none. Seems everyone is up to speed on their past life. Everyone except little Zephyr."

"Stop calling me that," I demanded. Those words were all I could manage as a defense. I really *didn't* remember much except that I got injected with whatever was in the syringe. Everything after that was blank. I tried not to show my frustration but I knew that I was failing. I wanted Satchel to tell me, to put the pieces together, but I didn't want to ask him to do it.

"And how did *you* die?" asked Lennox.

Satchel stood up and pulled the sleeves up to his elbows from his hoodie. "Let's try this: I'll explain everything I know and everything I did. But first—" he turned to me "—I want Zephyr to tell everyone what he did."

Was he trying to bargain? I knew what he wanted but I wasn't giving in. "You already know I don't remember."

He wasn't giving up. "Cut the crap, Zephyr. You know very well you do."

"You just explained to everyone here how I don't remember anything. Did you not?"

He was getting angry. He clearly hated everything about me and he was making sure that everyone here would hate me just as much. "Tell them," he demanded. "Tell them about Fletcher." Ugh. Why?! Satchel knew the story, didn't he? Why did he want *me* to be the one to tell it? I looked around at the lot, all of them now seemingly interested at what Satchel was requesting. Odds were against me, but defeated as I was, I wasn't giving up.

"Why?" I managed. I knew I was stalling, but I really didn't want to talk about Fletcher. The past was the past. Why couldn't Satchel let it be?

"Why not?" he countered. I knew he wasn't going to drop this, so I thought for a moment. Satchel said he was going to explain his side of things, meaning he was going to tell me how I died. Well, no, how he *killed* me.

I shuddered. "Because it's irrelevant."

Satchel chuckled. "You amaze me, you know that? You *actually* believe the things that come out of your mouth."

"I don't lie."

"Oh yeah, I forgot. You just don't tell the truth." I stared past him and everyone else up at the highway on top of the hill. It was useless trying to argue with Satchel. I could stall a little longer but we weren't going to make any progress if I did.

"Here's a truth," I started, "you're a murderer."

"Like you're so different?"

He struck a nerve. Was he actually comparing us? He'd just confessed to a triple homicide and he has the audacity to say I was no different? The balls this guy had. "I'm nothing like you," I clarified.

"Know what?" he continued, "you're right! If you were, we probably wouldn't be here!"

"Okay," intervened Lennox, "that's enough!" Satchel and I stopped talking at the interruption of Lennox's words. Neither of us turned to her, but she kept talking anyway. "In case you two have forgotten, we died. All of us did. That is an unfortunate and very messed up fact."

She made her way in between Satchel and me. Spotlight was on her now. "I for one am trying to put the pieces together. Axel manned up and explained to us how wrong his actions were. Satchel already said he would explain what he knows." She turned to face me. "Things you *obviously* don't know about." She turned back to Satchel for a reassurance. "Right?"

Satchel gave a sarcastic smirk. "It's what I said."

"Okay then"—back to me—"do you think you can put your pride aside for one second and just comply with us?"

I don't understand Lennox. Well, I understand what she wants me to do but this isn't how she approached Axel. What happened to all the sweetness she was giving him? How can she suddenly side with Satchel? How can she quickly trust someone who committed murder? I stared at her for a few beats before I spoke. "Go to hell, Lennox."

I turned on my heel and called back over my shoulder a clarification––"*All* of you." I wasn't going to bargain with any of them. How could she just want me to comply with my murderer's orders? I did want answers, but I figured I could find them in other ways. Satchel could tell them all about Fletcher's death. They could sit and tell stories about their deaths, too. I suddenly felt no interest in this group anymore. I was over them.

I walked past the car and heard Lennox say something. I don't know what. I paid no attention. What did stop me in my tracks was what I heard Satchel say, "He *killed* Fletcher."

Part of me wanted to keep walking and let them say whatever they pleased. The other part of me wanted to turn around and clear my name. Of course, Satchel thought I killed Fletcher. But how could he accuse me of something he was never even present at? He wasn't there when Fletcher died, nor was he anywhere to be seen on the day of his funeral. Now, a year later, he shows up and starts throwing accusations my way? I couldn't just walk away from this.

I turned to face them again. "Fletcher was my best friend."

"Bullshit," spat Satchel. "You wanted him gone."

"Sorry, last I checked, Fletcher *killed* himself. Did he not?"

Satchel began making his way toward me. "Stop trying to act like you're so innocent, Zephyr. You know that you and all of your little robots you call friends are to blame."

This wasn't the first time I'd heard others refer to my friends as "robots." People called them that because I could get them to do whatever I wanted them to. Not only that, I changed their appearances to better suit their lifestyles as my friends. I never saw anything wrong that. Every groups needs a leader after all. Besides, I didn't change them to cause them harm, I changed them so they could better themselves.

Satchel looked past me. "Speaking of which, here's one now." I whipped my head around to see who he was referring to. There, standing a few feet from me was Tristan. I couldn't believe my eyes. Tristan was here! Seeing him before me instantly brought flashbacks of Tristan at my house. Tristan lying in a pool of blood. Tristan *dead*.

Tristan looked dazed. He wore the same dark jeans and sleeveless red and black patterned flannel shirt that he'd had on the last time I'd seen him. His hair was different, though. His brown bangs were combed up to an angle instead of all over the place when he last showed up at my house. His light skin at least had natural color rather than the paleness of looking like death, which made his freckles less noticeable.

"Tristan?" I tried. He didn't answer. He looked at me then over to the others. Then I remembered him at my house. He wanted to tell me something. Something had him so freaked, so scared. Well here he was and hopefully he could tell me. But then I wondered if questioning him about that night was the right way to approach him right now, probably not. How long had he been standing there anyway? I came down the hillside and even climbed up the second floor of the factory. I was bound to have seen him somewhere.

"Tristan?" I tried again. "Hey, dude, can you hear me?"

He looked at me for a few seconds before turning to Satchel. "That's a lie."

What? What was he talking about? Tristan had this sort of thing for summing up everything before him in one word before explaining himself. Was he listening to everything we were just talking about just now? How long has he even been here?

"Zanniel didn't kill Fletcher," he continued. "Fletcher hung himself, Satchel. You *know* that. We all explained it to you. You're just looking for someone to blame."

We? Okay, he lost me. "What are you talking about? When did you talk to him?"

"At the hospital," he managed after a few seconds without taking his eyes off Satchel. Hospital? What hospital? Last I checked, none of my friends ever mentioned anything about seeing Satchel anywhere. What was Tristan talking about?

"I guess your robot here isn't as loyal to you as I thought," said Satchel. "I was more than positive that he ran to you after meeting up with me to tell you everything." So, he *had* seen Satchel before I did. But when? How? More importantly, why?

Tristan didn't answer him. Instead, he pulled me by my arm away from the others and spoke in a low voice once out of ear shot. "Is it true?" he whispered.

"Is what true?"

"All that stuff you guys were talking about, the death stuff. I heard you guys talking back there and over in downtown. It all makes sense but I mean, come on, Zanniel. Dead? Are we really dead?"

"That was you?" So, Tristan was the one who I had seen before. Well, that answered that. "Why did you run from me?"

"I don't know, okay? I was scared, confused… I still am."

I looked over at the others. They didn't look like they were conversing. They were all looking our way. Probably waiting for us to get back and acknowledge them. Lennox especially. I turned back to Tristan. "Yes. It's true. I'm not sure how, but it is. I saw you dead, dude. You were laying on the floor with a bunch of blood under you. *Your* blood." Tristan just stared at me, taking in what I'd just told him. I don't know exactly how he died, but I was certain he did. Seeing him in front of me just proved it even more.

I felt like now was the time to ask. "Hey, before we were attacked. You were going to tell me something. I tried forcing it out of you, but you got attacked before you could speak. Do you remember?"

He was giving me the same look he did on our last night alive. He looked freaked and scared, but this time he was going to tell me one way or another. "Spit it out, Tristan. You're hiding something."

He swallowed hard. "It's double-crossing."

I leaned in closer. "What is?"

"What they did, Zanniel. *All* of them. I don't get it. We were all best friends…" He trailed off but I know I heard him correctly.

"Stop beating around the bush, Tristan. Just say it already."

Tristan sighed. "They came after us. They helped Satchel."

"Who did?"

"Our friends did. Zanniel, they all wanted you dead."

VII

UNLEASHED

WHAT WAS IT ABOUT ME exactly that apparently had others wanting me dead? Okay, so Satchel held a grudge against me for what happened to Fletcher. But my friends? What the hell?! No, I take that back. Those leaches are not worthy of being referred to as my *friends*. Friends don't go around killing each other. Talk about ungrateful! It was thanks to me that they got to live the privileged lives they did in high school. See, I helped make every one of their sorry, boring, and pitiful existences into the perfect, rich and high-class beings that everyone liked to call my "robots." But together, we were known as the "Savage Seven."

Kalvin. Or better known as "Red" because he was the only naturally red-haired guy in the whole school. We met during physical ed. our freshman year. Red already had looks and talents all on his own prior to my upgrades. The guy was a pro at baseball and soccer and he did turn a few heads in the halls. The main problem with Red was that the boy had no self-confidence. Nor did he ever really converse with anyone. We split up into two teams during class that year while playing soccer, and with him on my side, we dominated everyone else. Shortly after, I took him under wing. I made him try out for sports with me. I also helped make him several social media accounts to get him to socialize more. With shout outs from my social media and just my friendship all together, he was instantly on the popularity list. But Red was still more than stupid when it came to girls. I took him to a party one night where he hooked up with not one, not two, but three different girls in one night. As awesome as that sounds to any guy who thinks with his dick rather than his brain, Red's little stunt got him infected with both herpes and chlamydia in the same night. Being the good friend I was, I was the one who took him to get tested in the first place after he had bailed on Fletcher and me several times because he was in "pain." After a few lectures on what condoms were and how to use them, he stopped letting his testosterone get the better of him. He still had hook ups now and then, but he knew better than to not use condoms.

Jason. This black haired and blue-eyed party animal, was always throwing get-togethers. Whether it was a bon fire, kick-back, party, or a gathering to celebrate an event of some sort, he was always the host. I had known of him all freshman year. Not because we were close, but because he was the only male in the school dance team. It wasn't until wrestling season of our sophomore year that we began classifying each other as friends. Funny how that ended up happening. During one of his parties, Jason had a little too much to drink. I never understood where he got the information that getting trashed at your own party was okay; It wasn't. Needless to say, he got a bad case of alcohol poisoning that night. Out of all the other people at that party, I was the one that cut him off and drove him to the emergency room. Well, Red, Tristan and Fletcher were there, too. But it was my idea. The next day, he couldn't stop telling me how thankful he was that I had saved him. Not that I minded, but he was the one that started hanging out with me and my friends after that. He would tag along during lunch, after practice, and even on the weekends. Aside from that, any party he was throwing, I was the first to know. Jason also learned how to have more fun at his parties because of the way I would pull drinks out of his hands, keeping him sober. He didn't complain, he just knew I was looking out for him.

Nolan. Me and him and his bleached emo-bangs and exaggerated acne go way back to seventh grade when he was a transfer student from a different district. Back then, he hated my guts. He would often call me out on things like being unfair, rude, selfish, or anything of similar matter. Quite the crybaby if you ask me. He didn't do it with the intention of bettering himself or him winning against me in any way. He just didn't want the spotlight to always be on me. It wasn't until basketball season our freshman year that he learned to keep his mouth shut. That year, all of our peers, including myself, were shooting hoops for the varsity team after tryouts while he sat low rank on C-team. How sad, not to even get a spot on junior varsity. Nolan knew I had favoritism from the coach and I knew how much he loved the sport. He pulled me aside after the rosters had been posted and begged me to talk to our coach about reconsidering his spot. I laughed in his face 'cause I knew how pathetic his situation was. After watching him literally grovel at my feet for a few minutes, I did end up talking to coach. With my persuasive reasoning, Nolan would be playing at our first game for the varsity team. Since that favor, he never had anything bad to say toward me ever again. Well, maybe he still did. But I figured he bit his tongue instead.

Clemont. The smartest robot of them all, not to mention our class's valedictorian. Now, when I say smart, I mean book-smart, not people-smart. While getting straight As is necessary to be successful throughout school, one also needs to have a social life outside of class. Not for success, but for sanity reasons. Clemont was my lab partner in chemistry class during sophomore year. As our projects and class work got done with ease (mostly because Clemont preferred to do most of work, ensuring we got a good grade), we had a lot of free time. During which I convinced him to have clothes in his closet other than graphic tees and cargo shorts. I also got him to dye his blond bangs black, the opposite of what Nolan had. Getting Clemont to change his appearance was an easy task. It was getting him to socialize that was the real challenge. While he did agree to hang out with me and the guys outside of class, he mostly just sat there and listened to our conversations. Clemont was so enclosed in his own shell that he wouldn't open up to any of us. We were never sure if he was upset, mad, happy or any other emotion. He had such a serious face all the time. He would answer when spoken to but he wouldn't hold up the conversation. It wasn't until he asked me how to shoot a basketball one random evening that I finally found common ground with him. Behind his glasses and overall nerd factor, he just wanted to be one of us: a jock. I got him to try out for several sports that year but the only team he ended up making was track. Not that he was good at it, but track never cut anyone. But it was a start. We trained long and hard that summer, building plenty of muscle over his too-skinny physique. Sure enough, it was varsity from football season on.

Tristan. This freckled-face and I grew up on the same street, but it wasn't until early freshman year that we became friends. While I was involved in sports, school activities, and just living my perfect life all together, Tristan was the doing the exact opposite. After CYFD took him away from his parents in middle school, his grandma took on the role of his guardian. But that's all she had for it: the title. Tristan was one of those kids who skipped school, vandalized property, and just hung out with the wrong crowd most of the time. Always at the skate park, with skateboards, but never skating for some odd reason. He had guidance, but he chose to be a rebel instead. Driving home one day, I saw him limping, looking like he had just been attacked by dogs. Dirty body, busted lip, trashed clothes, and several bruises. He refused my ride at first, but gave in by my second offer. I didn't even have to ask what happened to him. Once he got in the car, he poured out all his problems he had bottled up inside: his family, failing school, doing drugs, and the most recent story about getting jumped. He had scabs and scars around his wrists that he chose not to mention, but I put the pieces together myself. For the first time, I felt sorry for someone. Not just pity, but I felt the need to help. No, to *save* this individual. All I could offer at the time was my friendship, and as it turns out, that's all he really needed. He retired his skateboard (not that I ever saw him use it) and ditched his old friends. I helped him get his grades up so he would eventually join sports with me the following year. I got him to cut his shaggy brown hair, got him a sports watch and a few bracelets to cover his wrists, a few hand-me-downs from my closet (not that he minded one bit), and Tristan was a whole new person.

So many things I did for these guys out of the kindness of my heart. And in return, these bastards wanted me dead? Well, all except Tristan apparently. But why would he keep this from me? After everything I helped him get through, why not tell me? This isn't some middle school prank or some childish stunt. We're talking death. Last I checked, wanting to kill someone isn't healthy, not to mention sane.

I gave Tristan a shove and he stumbled backwards. "And you're telling me this now?" My shove caught him off guard. He looked at me with a defeated face and seemed at a loss for words. Of course, he was. What could he possibly say right now to make things better? Sorry? Forgive me?

"Okay," he tried. "Guilty. I'm totally guilty as a matter of fact."

"Damn straight," I agreed.

"No, please listen to me, Zanniel. Sure, they all talked about it, but I didn't think they would actually do it."

"Well obviously they did!" I pointed out.

"No! *Listen* to me, Zanniel. When you said you saw Satchel at UNM, that's when I knew that this was more than just a topic spoken about. That's when I knew that they we're actually coming for you."

He spoke quickly but I caught every word. That meant only one thing. "So, you're saying that the freaks with the masks that attacked us at my house, that was *them*?!"

I asked a question but I already knew the answer. Scenes from that night were flashing in my mind. They were so violent with me, not to mention even Tristan got caught in the middle. But why him? What did Tristan do to deserve death? Not that it really mattered now, but I began to wonder who was who? They all had masks on so I really had no idea. Who was in my room? Who threw me down the stairs? Better yet, whose head did I smash and whose thigh did I stab?

Tristan didn't answer but his expression answered for him. But I still had questions: why and how were my friends involved with Satchel to even begin with? After Fletcher killed himself, Satchel disappeared and now Tristan had said something about a hospital. There was definitely a lot more to be said than just this.

"Nice touch, huh?"

I whipped my head around saw Satchel standing before us with an accomplished look on his face. Clearly eavesdropping and looking very much pleased with himself. What could I say to him? I just found out that my group of friends were all backstabbers, but I knew that he already had knowledge of that.

"Tell me, Zephyr," he continued, "did it hurt?"

I stared at him with a straight but focused face. He's had the upper hand more often than I have and that had to stop. I wanted to just stay quiet since letting him talk would probably give me more than enough information to go on. I was a bit apprehensive to the fact that he was about to tell me details I wasn't fully prepared to hear.

"My blade?" he continued. "Tearing you open from one end to the other?" Satchel was insane. He had to be. Who in their right mind kills another human being and then asks them if it hurt? He showed no remorse or regret over the fact that he willingly took my life. He was the exact opposite. He seemed to be gloating, more than proud of his accomplishment.

"It really is a shame you don't remember," he taunted. "What a sight it was. My brother would've been proud to see that I took it upon myself to serve justice to the sorry being that he once worshipped." Back up. Fletcher killed *himself.* Why was Satchel so angry at *me*? Granted, Fletcher's death could've been prevented. But why was he so set on putting the blame on me?

"That's inaccurate," clarified Tristan. "Fletcher was our best friend. He never would've wanted any of this."

Satchel scoffed and turned his attention to Tristan. "Of course you would side with him. Out of all the other robots, you were the only one who just couldn't be reprogrammed. Call it loyalty, or friendship, or whatever the hell you want. I call it *weak*."

Tristan swallowed a big gulp but kept his cool. "That's an opinion." At least Tristan was on my side. But what about the others? Did everything I did for them mean nothing at all? I couldn't help but feel a little unappreciated.

Lennox made her way over to us. She must've gotten bored trying to get anything else out of Axel. We weren't that far from them. I was sure they'd heard everything. "As confusing as your situation is," she started, "here's what I've got so far:

"You, Zanniel, were the leader of your friends. Friends who all turned their backs on you. All except him." She gestured toward Tristan. "Somewhere in time, one of your friends killed himself: Fletcher. *The* Fletcher who also happened to be the brother of Satchel. Not sure why exactly they decided to turn on you but I'm guessing it had something to do with losing your friend. Enraged with anger and the need for revenge, Satchel felt the need to take matters into his own hands by eliminating the one he felt was responsible."

This chick was both nosy and annoying. She talked like she was a little miss know-it-all. Aside from that, I knew she wasn't stupid. She picked up all that with the very few things that were said? Talk about paying attention to detail.

She turned to Satchel for confirmation. "Am I off?"

Surprisingly, Satchel looked impressed. "Why, no. Actually, you're right on track."

Lennox breathed out a sigh of relief. "Okay, good. But there are a few things that are still unclear. You killed Zanniel. I mean, you made that perfectly clear, but did you kill Tristan as well?"

Satchel looked at Lennox, then to Tristan and back again. "Yes," he answered, "maybe not as brutal as Zephyr got it. But death all the same."

How can he say that so smoothly? I looked over at Tristan and his face looked shattered. He took a few deep breaths and then began to sob. Satchel may have hated me, but what did Tristan ever do?

"And, why did you?" asked Lennox. As pushy as she may be, she was the only one getting information out in the open. Satchel had agreed to tell his side of the story *only* if I told my part about what happened to Fletcher. It was a bargain that he now seemed to completely have forgotten about. But if he wasn't bringing it up again, I wasn't either.

"If I didn't," explained Satchel, "Zephyr here would've probably gotten away. All the other robots were easy to convince that eliminating him was the best thing to do. But I just couldn't seem to get through to that one."

Tristan's sobs grew louder. Not as loud as Axel's were, but loud enough to make it noted that he was in pain. Not physically of course, but emotionally. He put his hands behind his head and started pacing.

I couldn't keep quiet anymore, I had to speak up. I pulled Tristan by his flannel and hissed quietly, "Get a *grip*. Go cry over there." I pushed him back and he turned away from the others. I turned to Satchel. "You killed an innocent guy."

Satchel turned his head toward me. His brow furrowed and I got the feeling that he was about to unload more information on me. "And you didn't?!"

Here we go again. "*No.* I didn't."

He clenched his fists and began to shake. He let out a loud shriek that made us all jump.

"Of course. Of course!" he exclaimed. "All you bastards are exactly the same! None of you could come to terms with the fact that you're all equally responsible!" I took a step back. Satchel's rage had completely taken over. I braced myself for whatever was about to come.

"My brother deserved better! All he ever did was praise you, and you turned your back on him! All your stupid robots did! The only thing

I regret is not finishing off your sad little clan, Zephyr! The rest of the Savage Seven deserve to rot in hell just as much as you do!

"As sad as it is, you got the easy way out. You didn't feel an ounce of the pain that my brother did. The isolation, the betrayal. Not to mention the humiliation? You know none of that!

"You don't even know the pain *I* went through! I was down at Cruces when I heard about Fletcher's death. I got to Albuquerque only to get locked up for being unstable and dangerous. But come on! Could they blame me?! I lost my brother, my schooling, my sanity, my *life*!"

I glanced over at Lennox. She looked deep in thought as she listened to everything Satchel was throwing at me. You would think she would look startled or scared. But she seemed calm at his fury. I could speak up and stop Satchel's nonsense and accusations. After all, I already heard everything I needed to.

"One more question," said Lennox calmly after a few beats of nothing but heavy breathing from Satchel. "How did you die?" Yes! Finally, a useful question. How did he? Lennox seemed to get answers when she asked questions. All Satchel gave me was pointless rambling.

Satchel looked down at the ground and chuckled to himself. "Oh, I have *him* to thank for that. Don't I, officer?"

We all turned our attention over at Clyde, who hadn't said a single word during Satchel's barks. I almost forgot he was even still around. He was looking down at the white mask Satchel had worn. He held it in his hands and stared at it with intense focus. Not sure when exactly he went to pick it up, but he waited a few seconds before looking up at us.

Clyde's face was red with both shock and anger. I could see his chest expand with every deep breath he was taking before he finally spoke. "You rambunctious scamp!"

VIII

RISING

RAMBUNCTIOUS SCAMP...HMMM. NO IDEA WHAT Clyde meant by that. Sounded insulting, though. By the way his blue eyes were flaring and locked on Satchel, you would think he was about to attack. Talk about furious.

"Wait," said Lennox as she turned her attention to Clyde, "you killed Satchel?"

"Looks like it, don't it?" he replied. Ugh. So many twists and turns kept happening, I couldn't keep up. Earlier, when Clyde pulled Satchel away from me, Satchel had recognized him when he saw who had pulled him off. Clyde didn't have the same reaction, though. How did Satchel know that Clyde was the one who killed him? How *did* he kill him? Did all these events (my death, Axel's, Satchel's, and probably Clyde's, and Lennox's) happen at the same time? Well, not the same time, but the same night? They must have. How else and why else would we all be here? I know I have no evidence to back up my theory, but I felt like I was coming onto something.

At least Lennox was good at something: she kept filling in the blanks, so that kept *me* from being the one to ask questions. "Why didn't you say anything before?" she asked him.

Clyde's eyes never left Satchel's, nor did he let go of the mask. "Pardon me, sweetheart. But ah ain't gonna go 'round tellin' you folks who ah know nothin' 'bout who I've gone put bullets in." Oh, *shit*. No sugar-coating that one. Clyde said "bullets," so did that mean Satchel got shot? When? But, why is Clyde here then if he killed Satchel?

"'Course," he continued, "didn' know it was this one ah shot 'cause he was hidin' behind this mask. Ya' *coward*." He threw the mask on the ground. I turned to Satchel only to see he was giving Clyde a mocking grin. So that's why Clyde hadn't recognized him: Satchel had the mask on. Why did Clyde shoot him, though?

Before letting Lennox speak, I went ahead. "Besides obvious reasons, why did you shoot him? Don't get me wrong, good job for bringing this prick to justice, officer. But, what was going on that made you do so?" I wanted background information now.

"Personally," started Clyde, "ah reckon any yellow-belly runnin' 'round wearin' a mask *deserves* to be shot at. But this one here was off ma' radar goin' over a hundred in the interstate." So Satchel was speeding…and then he got shot? Maybe. I had to really focus whenever Clyde spoke. Not only did he speak kind of fast, but his accent didn't make it any easier. Not to mention his grammar: Reckon? Yellow-belly? Seriously, who talks like that?

"So, then these cars belong to you guys," said Lennox as she pointed to the cars parked in front of the factory. Cars that hadn't been there the first time I passed. I wondered if that was because the events Clyde was telling us about hadn't happened yet. It would make sense.

"Right," agreed Clyde, "soon as ah saw this one run some other car off the road, ah made sure he wasn' gettin' 'way." That "someone" was Axel. So, these events *did* happen one after another. Before Clyde continued talking, I put a few pieces together going off the things he was saying and what Lennox had said earlier: Satchel snapped, came after me, killing Tristan in the process, ran Axel off the road, then got shot by Clyde. Okay, all that makes perfect sense so far. But, how did Clyde die? And how was Lennox connected to all of this?

Satchel walked over to retrieve the mask that was thrown on the ground. "Long story short," he started, "Clyde here followed me ever since I left Tijeras. After my incident with Axel, I pulled off into a side road that led me here." He pointed to the factory with the mask. "And it was basically a game of cat and mouse after that."

"Yeah," continued Clyde, "ran off inside soon's he pulled in. Played a little hide-n-seek before comin' at me from behind." They talked to each other with tones of accusation. Satchel did speak more calmly, as Clyde had an edge to his voice. Clyde stood his ground with his arms crossed while Satchel paced in circles around us. I wasn't sure where Tristan wandered off to; he knew how I felt about crying. Axel went completely mute. Lennox on the other hand looked intrigued. You could tell by the thirst in her brown eyes that she wanted to hear more of Clyde and Satchel's encounter.

I couldn't deny the fact that I was a little interested in their killings as well. "Attacking while the other had his back turned?" I called out.

Satchel looked satisfied. "Survival of the fittest. Clyde, being the good cop that he was, had a gun on him. I had to plan my moves carefully." He stopped pacing and directed his words at Clyde. "And may I compliment you on your impressive endurance, officer. I stabbed you more than twenty times in your back before finally ramming my knife in your gut." He spoke like he was amazed that Clyde didn't die more quickly. It was probably all the muscle he had on him.

"Yeah, well," said Clyde, "unfortunately for you, ah got my gun jus' in time to get one blow through you. Looks like that's all it took."

Satchel threw him a mocking smile. Lennox ran her hands through her blonde hair before speaking. "So, you guys killed each other."

"Would've shot this prick sooner had it not been for him landin' on top of me, knockin' my gun outta ma' hands."

Satchel chuckled. "It was kind of funny watching a cop of your size literally crawl on the floor trying to save his life. Had you not reached your gun in time, it'd just be you standing here right now." Clyde didn't answer, he just glared at Satchel. Did he have no remorse? Or the slightest hint of regret for doing any of the things that he did? Body count: Me,

Tristan, Clyde, Axel, and Axel's brother. Five different murders in one night. Talk about insane.

I heard footsteps coming from behind. I glanced over and saw Tristan coming back to join us from wherever he went. His eyes were red from crying, and his cheeks were red, making his freckles stand out. Listening to the events that had happened between Clyde and Satchel got me thinking: if this *was* Limbo like Lennox was saying and we had yet to be judged, why was Tristan here? Was his keeping of the secret plot to kill me enough to deny him entering heaven?

What about Clyde? We still don't know anything more about him other than the fact that he killed Satchel. It's kind of funny, just when a cop manages to do something right for a change, he dies. Talk about sad. But what about beyond that? What bad deeds did he do that has him stuck in Limbo?

Lennox, too. She may be good when it comes to asking questions. But, she has a few of them coming her way from my part. Who was she exactly? How did *she* die? She looked innocent enough, so why was she not in heaven? Or hell, for that matter.

A few moments of silence passed by when I heard a voice. I whipped my head around half-expecting to see someone; I didn't. Everything was the same. I turned to Tristan to see if he had heard it, too. But, instead he just looked at my shocked expression with a confused one. He narrowed his eyes. "What is it?"

I waited a few seconds before answering. "Did you hear that?"

He raised an eyebrow; I took that as a no. I turned to the others. "Anyone?"

Lennox was the first to respond. "Hear what, exactly?"

"The voice?" I asked. Was she playing dumb? Did no one else hear it?

"Hearing voices, Zephyr?" asked Satchel. "Careful. Keep that up and people might think you're going crazy."

"You would know, right?" I countered. I waited and listened carefully. The others looked to be doing the same. Sure enough, I heard it again.

It sounded like a cry. I wasn't sure what it was saying or if it was even a guy or a girl. It was faint. But, it sounded closer than what it had before. Lennox gave a small gasp and that gave away that she heard it as well.

"Benny?" whispered Axel. He looked alert and was quick on his feet. He began looking frantically looking around. "Benny!"

It got a little harder to focus on where the voice was coming from with Axel's sudden shouts and echoes. Everyone started looking in all different directions. So far, no one saw anyone else besides us. As I looked around, I noticed a shift in the fog that was surrounding us. It looked like it was moving.

I heard the voice call out again, this time more clearly. "Ax!" it called out. Ax, I was assuming, was short for Axel.

"Benny!" shrieked Axel. "I'm right here, Benny! I'm right here!"

A gust of wind moved through us. Lennox's blonde hair moved across her face and Axel placed a hand on his hat, pressing it down to keep it from blowing away. The sudden wind had me on edge. What was happening? I looked around and finally spotted something: a boy. Past the crashed car and on top of the hill the others and I climbed down from, there he stood. He wore a white hat, white jacket and pants with white shoes.

"Ax!" he called down to us. I glanced over at Axel and he looked like he'd just seen a ghost. Well, maybe he did. What *was* Benny? A spirit? An angel? More importantly, where did he come from? And why did he choose to show up *now*?

He climbed down the hill with ease. As he got to the bottom, he ran toward us. I saw not only the overjoy on his face, but a wide smile, and the striking resemblance he had to Axel. He had a lot of the same facial features and he was even wearing the same thing that Axel was. Except Benny had the opposite color.

"Ax!" he called out again. Axel stood motionless. Even when Benny finally reached him and threw himself on him, Axel just wrapped his arms around him. His shocked expression didn't change. I looked over at the others and saw that they were just as surprised. Okay, so the last time Axel saw Benny was when he died. It was understandable why *he* would be in such shock to hold him again. But everyone else? Why were *they* so shocked? They didn't even know Benny. Why were they so surprised to see him? Clyde had his arms crossed over his chest and for some odd reason, the others did too. They were all quiet. Probably waiting eagerly to see what happened next.

I guess Lennox was too shocked by the sudden visit, as she hadn't said a single thing. Looked like I'd have to be the one to ask questions now. "Where did you come from, kid?"

"Benny," whispered Axel, "I'm so sorry…"

"For what?" responded Benny. He looked so alive, so happy. Did he not know he was dead? I also noted that he had completely ignored my question.

"For everything," answered Axel. His eyes started to gather tears and the sobs began once more. Okay, we get it! You're upset. Enough with the crying.

"You're so weird!" exclaimed Benny. "Hurry up! We gotta go, Ax! I have lots to show you!" Go? Go where? What was this kid talking about? There was nowhere to go.

"Wait a sec," I tried again. "Go where?"

"Okay," whispered Axel, "you can show me whatever you want." He put Benny down gently. Why was this kid not answering me? Axel took Benny by the hand and started walking back toward the hill where Benny was first seen.

"Whoa, whoa, whoa!" I shrieked. "Dude, Axel, where exactly are you going?"

"It's so cool!" continued Benny. "It's like those video games we played, Ax! Only cooler!" Why were they not answering me? Damn it! I hated when I got ignored. I walked toward them. I had to stop them, get some information out of this kid. I reached for Axel's shoulder to turn him around but my hand went right through him.

My jaw dropped. It was like Axel was a hologram or something. "Axel?" I froze and just stared at them as they walked away.

Once they passed the broken car, they stopped, and Benny pointed to the top of the hill past the highway. "It's just up there!" he exclaimed. The wind that had picked up around us seemed to be going in a circle. First it was gentle, then it started to pick up speed. Loose gravel, pieces of glass and car scraps got picked up in the circular drift. I got the feeling as if I was inside a hurricane of some sort. I looked around at the others but they looked just as confused.

"Zanniel?!" I heard Tristan call out. I didn't answer. I, myself, was trying to make sense of what was going on. I stared through the winds at Axel and Benny. Still hand in hand, they seemed not to notice the bizarre change in our surrounding climate. As I looked out, a bright flash came out of nowhere that blinded me. I shielded my eyes and even let out a small grunt. The blinding light didn't hurt to see. It was just uncomfortable.

I stood motionless for a second before I decided to try and open my eyes. I slowly opened them and they adjusted rather quickly. When I saw that the flash was gone, I realized Axel had changed. His entire wardrobe was radiating in bright whites just like Benny's was. Everything from his hat to his shoes looked like it was practically glowing.

Axel looked back over his shoulder and his face was different as well. The was no longer any sadness or a single dull feature left on his facial expression. The exact opposite of that, he looked happy. He was smiling and his eyes didn't show any sign that they had been shedding tears. I would've never guessed that the guy standing a few feet away was the same guy I encountered downtown. The winds slowly subsided and everything was quiet.

"You ready?!" asked Benny.

Axel turned his attention back to his brother and nodded in agreement. "I'm ready." He squatted down, and in one swift motion he propped Benny on his back like a piggyback ride. Axel took one step forward after standing up straight, and then another bright flash illuminated everything once more. The light was harsh and as much as I tried to keep my eyes open, I couldn't.

A few beats passed and I slowly opened my eyes again only to realize that both Axel and Benny were gone. My eyes scanned the scene, but there was no one there anymore. As I looked closer, the car and all the mess that came from it was gone, too. Everything relating to Axel had vanished. It looked as though he was never even here.

So, now what? Axel was gone. He probably crossed over, like Lennox had theorized. But, was it heaven he went to? It had to be. I doubted that going to hell would require him dressing in full white attire. Plus, he looked so *happy*. With that thought in mind, what did this mean for the rest of us?

Though no trace of Axel was left, a white dove flying in the sky caught my eye. I wasn't entirely sure if it had anything to do with Axel, so I just stared quietly as it flapped its wings. So out of place this dove was, bight and white, soaring in a gloomy dark sky. I didn't look back at the others, though I was more than positive that they were all staring at it, too. Staring as it flew away from us and eventually disappeared into the sky.

IX

BREAKPOINT

THE SILENCE LASTED A FEW moments. What could any of us say? Bye, Axel? Take care? This didn't feel real. Things like this didn't happen. This felt like something you see in a movie or something. If I wasn't giving into the whole "Limbo" theory before, I gave now.

I stared up at the sky a few more moments before attempting to break the silence. I didn't have to look around at the others to know that they were in as much shock as I was. So that was heaven? I mean, what exactly did Axel do that made his final judgment, like Lennox said, be decided?

Well, why not ask Lennox? I mean, she was the one that pitched this whole idea about crossing over in the first place. Let's see what she had to say now. I turned around and locked eyes with Lennox. "What the hell was that?"

She looked slightly startled when she heard my voice. "What do you mean?"

"Exactly what I asked."

She looked distracted. I really didn't blame her. I kept seeing that bright flash everywhere I turned. And what was up with the hurricane thing we were just in? That came out of nowhere. I looked over at Tristan only to find him awestruck with his mouth hung open. Both Clyde and Satchel stared up motionless as well. Was I the only one that was already past the little event that had just taken place?

"Well?" I asked her.

She played with her hands as she looked down at the ground. She finally had nothing to say. Ha! Well, spotlight's on her now. I felt like now was the time to try to get information about her. "Know what? Forget what just happened. Let's talk about you."

"Me?" She sounded surprised. What, did she think she was just going to get by without disclosing any of her dirty little secrets?

"Yes." I mocked her tone. "You."

"What about me?"

Funny how she was trying to play dumb. She knew exactly what I was getting at. Tristan could probably shed more light on Satchel, and Clyde was next on my list for questions. Satchel could go to hell now for all I care. Lennox needed to start answering all the questions I had about her. "We know nothing about you, Lennox. Tell us, how'd you get here?"

I remember back in downtown she said something about a "he." She had all her memories—I was sure of it. I was expecting her to just bust out with her entire life story but instead she just gave a flat "No."

My brow furrowed. "No? Why the hell not?"

"Because," she started, "I don't owe you any kind explanation. Not until you tell us about Fletcher. I haven't forgotten the bargain." Wow. She told me. My words got caught in my mouth. I knew she was right about me not talking about Fletcher. But still, what's the point?! She already knew Satchel murdered me, she didn't need to know the minor details.

"What do you want to know?" asked Tristan. I turned to see him heading toward us. Tristan was there throughout Fletcher's death. He could tell the story just as clear as I could. Or could he? I wasn't too sure anymore, seeing as how Tristan managed to keep secrets from me. For all I knew, he could have been involved with my murder, just as much as the others were. I never doubted Tristan's loyalty. It felt strange to have to be cautious with him.

He caught Lennox off guard. It was all over her face. "Just answers. Maybe a little better understanding of why Satchel hates Zanniel so much. You know, besides the obvious." She wasn't asking much, but I doubt Tristan would go into detail about *exactly* what went down our senior year. Would he?

"Ask away," he instructed.

I never liked others to talk for me but Tristan seemed eager, almost like he wanted to prove himself to me or something. "You don't have to tell her anything," I told him.

"It's fine," he assured me. "Go." If Lennox was wanting Tristan to just start talking about everything he knew, she had another thing coming. It was a little hilarious watching Tristan act tough toward Lennox. Probably because I knew that his bark was worse than his bite. But Lennox *did* seem a little intimidated. This should be interesting.

I heard Satchel laugh lightly. "Zephyr can't speak for himself?"

"That's irrelevant," countered Tristan. "She wants to know about Fletcher. Don't think it makes a difference as to who tells the information. Does it?" He was talking to Lennox now, who looked a little hesitant.

"No." She was trying so hard to stay composed. "I suppose it doesn't."

It sounded like Satchel mumbled "whatever." I glanced over at Clyde who was just staring at the ground with his arms crossed. He was listening to us, no doubt about it.

"Well?" asked Tristan. Tristan amazed me. He used to be the pushover type when I first befriended him. Shortly after I helped his life get back in order, he grew a backbone. He took a few pointers from watching me handle things, which was fine by me. I appreciated the admiration and determination.

Lennox took a deep breath. "What happened to Fletcher?"

"He hung himself."

Lennox gave a small grunt. "I know *that*."

"Then why'd you ask again?"

I tried so hard to contain my laugh. Tristan was acting like a dick to Lennox on purpose. Technically he wasn't wrong. He did answer her question after all. Lennox shot him a disapproving look. "*Why* did he hang himself?"

"Because the whole school found out his secret."

"Which was?" I could tell Lennox was getting irritated at Tristan's short answers. But she was eager to find out. She looked more than willing to put up with it.

"Not really sure. Either he was full-blown gay, or he had a gay crush on Zanniel." Suddenly, the humorous tone to Tristan's answers was gone. I remembered now, looking back at that day, I never told Tristan the *whole* story. Not him or any of my friends.

"What?" Lennox sounded surprised. What was she expecting? Not that there was anything wrong with being gay. My high school had a LGBTQ program and was always reaching out to students about loving themselves and all that sentimental bullshit. However, being gay was not heard of around me or any of my friends.

"What?" mimicked Tristan.

"How did your whole school get word about his sexuality?"

Tristan looked like he was choosing his words carefully. He was probably trying to word out an explanation in which I didn't end up looking like the bad guy. I stepped in. "Because I told them."

Lennox turned to me with a jaw-dropping expression. "Why would you expose a secret that's not yours?"

I shrugged my shoulders. "Fletcher was in the closet. I didn't see anything wrong with getting him to come out." That was a lie. But, there was no need for Lennox to know that.

"Do you have any idea the emotional impact that type of situation can have on a person?" Here we go again with the lectures. What was the point of talking about it now? Fletcher killed himself over a year ago. It was done. *I'd* moved on. Why shouldn't I have? I might have exposed his secret to the entire student body. But, in the end, it was him that had chosen to end his life, not me.

Tristan stepped in again. "Are your questions done now?"

"No, actually," she said irritability. "I'm just getting started. How exactly did you tell the whole school about it?"

"School newspaper," replied Tristan. It sounded childish, I know. Newspapers were a thing of the past. But I had a real passion for journalism. I got a thrill when it came to uncovering information. And who better to tell everyone about it than me? I joined journalism class my freshman year, and the senior editor at the time was just awful. His articles revolved around test scores, our school lacking sportsmanship, how students were encouraged to recycle… Seriously, who gives a shit? *All* the articles were about pointless topics.

Toward the end of my freshman year, I wrote an article about the importance of cliques and groups at our school and almost every student at Rio Grande High read it. Even the faculty gave me so much praise about approaching an often-overlooked topic. From the next school year on, *I* was head of the journalism program as the new editor. All my articles were front page news. My friends weren't really into journalism but they joined our junior year. They contributed to what they could, whether it be getting photos, topics, or even just being part of the printing process. During that year, it seemed everyone else prior was too intimidated having the Savage Seven join the class. So they all resigned their positions and left me and my friends to run the whole thing by ourselves.

"You're kidding," she said. She didn't sound convinced. I didn't want to go into details of how my newspaper articles impacted the school. Don't get me wrong, I have no problem talking about what amazing writing skills I have and the influence I had on others. But, what I really wanted right now was to know about Lennox. I had the slight suspicion that she was hiding something. Just like a journalist would, I *had* to find out.

"That's not a question," said Tristan. "But no. Everyone at school read Zanniel's paper. He had the voice and everyone lent their ears." As flattered as I should feel by Tristan's words, I still couldn't rid myself of the feeling that he was hiding things from me. I'd probably get answers from him eventually. But, I wanted to deal with Lennox first.

"Okay," she continued, "how did Zanniel even find out Fletcher was gay? There were several reasons why I knew, but I'd never disclosed all of them to anyone. "At a party at our friend Jason's, after we took state for basketball our senior year against La Cueva, we decided to celebrate. Fletcher was a little drunk and not only *told* Zanniel how he felt about him, but he made a move and tried to make out with him too."

On point, Tristan. I remembered that night so perfectly. While Fletcher was disclosing his feelings, and planting one on me, I was too distracted to notice that Tristan had come up behind us. Not only did he hear, but saw he saw the whole thing. I did notice that Tristan left out the part about him being drunk during the events.

"I saw it all," continued Tristan. "I even took a picture of it on my phone. There were even a few texts sent back and forth from them talking about it. A few screenshots, and they served as proof for the article being legitimate."

Lennox looked like she was in shock. Was she done with the questions? Tristan looked satisfied with the answers he'd given. Though she didn't ask, Tristan kept going. "Fletcher didn't meet us that morning. Zanniel told him we weren't going to journalism class. When Fletcher *did* get to school, everyone already had a paper in hand. Little did he know, everyone in the school knew something he didn't. Didn't take long for him to notice what was going on. Poor dude left school in a flash. Couldn't handle what was going on."

Lennox still didn't say anything. What more information could she possibly want? Clyde didn't say anything. I looked over at Satchel and saw the sour look on his face. Must be all the talk about his brother. Well, he asked for it!

"Anything else?" Asked Tristan. Lennox was in a daze. There was a light breeze that moved her hair over her face, but she didn't seem to notice. Was she still with us? I thought back to Axel and how he stopped acknowledging us. Was the same thing now happening with Lennox?

Before I got a chance to say anything else, she found her voice. "Wait, backtrack a little. Go back to this party if yours."

"I can't," said Tristan. "It happened over a year ago."

Tristan could be a bit of a smart ass at times. He did a good job picking it up after me. But he didn't always know when to stop. "What about it?" I asked her.

"Your state game against La Cueva, what school were you playing for?"

Was she serious? Tristan just told her everything that happened with Fletcher, and she stops to get details about a game and a party? "Rio Grande," said Tristan.

"What year did you graduate?" Her breathing had picked up. She looked a little scared, but I hadn't the slightest idea why. My brow furrowed and so did so did Tristan's.

"2016," I responded. "What does that have to do with anything?"

Lennox realized something just now. Her jaw dropped and eyes widened. "Oh, my god," she breathed. "I was there."

She was there? How? Why? That game happened over a year ago. Even if she *was* there, what did that have anything to do with Fletcher?

"So?" questioned Tristan.

"*So,*" she continued, "that's our connection!"

"It was the state basketball championships, half of Albuquerque was there." Tristan had a point. It was a long shot to believe that Lennox being at basketball game had any real significance.

"Oh, my god!" she said again with more excitement. "Don't you get it?!"

"No," Tristan and I said in unison. I understood what she was getting at but I didn't think there was any reason to be so excited about it.

"Okay," she breathed. "*I* was at that game. I was a cheerleader for La Cueva! After our team lost that game, I went to the after-party with my friends. My friend Trinity dragged me and our other friend Destiny along. Trinity was dating some guy from Rio and we just *had* to go with her. We never actually met the guy. He broke up with her and left before we got to meet him.

"But that's not the point! That's the first night I met Jason, too! It wasn't until this past summer that we actually started dating. That was his house, right? The party?"

"You know Jason?" Asked Tristan. Lennox threw a major curveball. She was at the basketball game *and* the party where Fletcher kissed me? Interesting. We were under the same roof twice and never crossed paths. Another thing she mentioned, "Trinity." Trinity was the cheerleader from Cueva I was dating back then who I broke up with that night. Could it be? Could it really be that Lennox and I were so closely connected? That's impossible! No. I'm just jumping to conclusions. There's no way.

"Well, yeah," replied Lennox. "He *was* my fiancé."

"No fucking way," I said, "Jason?!" Lennox looked offended. Even Tristan looked shocked when I turned to him. Did he not think this was just as hilarious as I did? Jason was the biggest party animal I knew. Kudos to him for finding a good-looking chick like Lennox. But seriously? I found this so funny that I started letting out chuckles just thinking about it. "You married Jason?!"

Of course, Jason and I weren't that close anymore after high school, which would explain why I never got to meet Lennox. I continued laughing, and Lennox lost all the excitement she just had a few seconds ago.

"Actually, *no*," she spat. "In case you haven't noticed, this bride isn't going to be walking down the aisle. I *died* remember?" She died…the rehearsal dinner! That's where I was supposed to be the night Satchel killed me! Jason's random invite to his event didn't seem so random anymore. Like Tristan said, my friends wanted me gone. Jason knew I was leaving Albuquerque that night. He kept me behind on purpose! He gave me a reason to stay longer so Satchel had enough time to come for me! It all fit so perfect. I wasn't laughing anymore. The sudden realization had me enraged.

"Speaking of death," I accused, "it's Jason's fault I'm even dead in the first place! The whole timing on your stupid wedding revolved around *me*. Jason wanted me dead just like the rest of my stupid friends. So he planned this so I would stay long enough to get murdered!"

Those were harsh and serious accusations I was throwing her way, but I knew I wasn't wrong. Lennox looked like she didn't have a clue as to what I was talking about. Satchel on the other hand was enjoying this. I heard him bust out laughing after I was done speaking. He started clapping his hands and made his way toward me yelling, "Ding! Ding! Ding! We have a winner!"

We all turned to Satchel. He looked overjoyed at my sudden discontent. How could I have been this stupid to not leave? Why did I have to stay? Ugh! I was ready to start punching Satchel in the face to wipe that smile off. But, I knew my blows would do no damage. Still, it would help take my anger out.

"Zephyr figured it out!" He announced to everyone, "The robots turned on their creator and it's *hilarious*. They all had their own contribution you know. Want to know how?"

"*No*," I spat. I really didn't want to hear anymore. I already knew those idiots helped with my murder. That was enough.

"Jason planned his wedding as a way to prolong your departure," he continued anyway. "Clemont made some special concoction that would paralyze you but keep you awake."

"Shut up, Satchel!"

"Red helped break me out of the hospital. Working at the front desk, a little file forging, and I practically walked out the front door."

"*Shut up!*"

"Nolan, wasn't much help in the *planning* of it all. But, he did know how to kill the lights at your place." I was clenching my teeth and I felt my body shaking with anger. He knew he was pissing me off and he knew how hard his words were hitting me. To hear how my friends contributed to my killing, it hurt. My feelings were actually being *hurt* by words. That was new. When I was alive, words were *my* weapon. *I* knew how to use them to get what I wanted. The words of others meant nothing to me. Their insults, judgement, criticism, all that and *more* never bothered me; not once. But this? This was something different. It was more than his words getting to me, I just didn't know what.

"Of course," he continued, "I made sure *I* was the one to actually erase you completely."

"Hey, wait," said Tristan. "Weren't you smashing some chick named Trinity from Cueva?" Funny how he didn't take note of anything that Satchel just explained. But he was right about Trinity. He confirmed what I was just thinking: the party, the break up, it was *her*. I knew Albuquerque was small but I didn't think it was *that* small. To have a connection with someone like Lennox by the means of Jason *and* Trinity. That was more than just a coincidence.

"*What?*" exclaimed Lennox.

"Yeah, yeah, yeah," continued Tristan, "I remember her. Blonde, cheerleader. You dumped her that night at Jason's."

"Wait, *WHAT?!*"

"Uh-oh," mocked Satchel, "Zephyr's in trouble."

"You were the asshole who broke Trinity's heart?!" she accused as she took fast steps toward me. Was she seriously standing up for a friend a year later? What did it matter?

"So what if I was?" I challenged.

Lennox looked like she had just been slapped. I'd seen Lennox upset, shocked, and irritated. But, this was the first time I saw her *angry*. She let out a loud grunt as she pressed her hands on my chest and shoved me backwards. It wasn't her strength that knocked me over, the stumbling had more to do with it. Either way, I found myself on my back looking up at the others. "You *bitch*! What is wrong with you?!"

"*You*," she snarled, "and people like you!"

"What are you barking about?" She lost me. She was clearly upset. But, why? What did my break up with Trinity have to do with her? It happened so long ago that I had almost forgotten about it completely. Surprised Tristan still remembered.

"This is all *your* fault!"

My fault? I was so lost. I was about start arguing with her when something on the ground past them caught my eye. It was Clyde. He was on the ground on his back. His body was twitching and he was flailing frantically like he was having some sort of seizure. Not only that, he seemed to be vanishing and reappearing in his place.

The others saw my shocked expression and turned to Clyde. When he was there, it looked like electric shocks were moving throughout his body. When he vanished, the electric shocks would stay, moving in his silhouette, but his body would no longer be visible. What was happening? One moment he was there, another he was gone. I thought back to Axel and how things were when he crossed over. It was nothing like this. Was Clyde going to hell? Part of me didn't think so, but then again, I had no idea how this Limbo place worked.

I saw a hand in front of me and realized it was Tristan offering to help me up. I grabbed it and got to my feet. No one said anything. Not that there was much to say. We all stared helplessly as Clyde was having his episode. I looked closer at Clyde's face and saw his eyes rolled to the back of his head and he looked to be grasping for air.

Lennox turned to us and broke the silence. "You guys," she breathed. "I don't think he's dead."

X

STEALTH

ONE YEAR AND SOME MONTHS ago.

"We won, Zanniel!" exclaimed Fletcher. "We beat Cueva!"

Fletcher was the most excited about our win. We all crammed into my Suburban, Fletcher sat shotgun and everyone else in the back. It was a close game: 64 to 62. The last game of our senior year and we took home the blue. Now it was time to celebrate with an after-party at Jason's, like always.

I felt my phone vibrate in my pocket. When I glanced at it I had a new text from Trinity. She and I hadn't been seeing each other that long and she was already on my last nerve. She would constantly blow my phone up with random texts about how she misses me, what I'm doing, that she loves me… I ignored half of them. It wasn't even love that she was feeling, it was infatuation. I certainly didn't love the chick. I was just passing the time. She was at the game tonight cheering for her school but I heard her cheer for me mostly.

"Is Trinity coming tonight?" asked Jason. "She was watching you like a hawk all night, dude."

Ugh. Even my friends noticed how obsessed she was. "I don't know, maybe." I didn't even want to be with her anymore. We were just friends at first then after we went on one date, she was hooked. How could girls get so clingy and get attached so quickly?

"You get enough bottles for tonight?" I asked back, trying to steer the conversation into a different direction.

"You know I always do," replied Jason. I knew. I was just looking for anything else to talk about. We talked about the game and other random stuff. No more Trinity-talk and I was thankful. I dropped off the other guys at their houses to get ready for the party. Fletcher and I were going to get ready at my place and he would crash at my place afterwards. We wore the same size. He would just borrow a few of my things for the night.

When we got to my house, my parents weren't home. Talk about workaholics. I showered in the upstairs bathroom and Fletcher showered in the downstairs. After I was done, I started looking for something to wear in my closet, wearing only boxer briefs. I was the most comfortable out of all my friends with my body. I was looking at myself in the mirror when Fletcher walked in.

"You know what sucks?" I asked as I flexed my upper body.

"What?"

"We never work upper body in basketball. We do mostly cardio."

"If you say so," he replied nervously. Fletcher always got a little uncomfortable when I was shirtless. His body tone wasn't as defined as mine but he still looked good. Even now, he had on a T-shirt covering his body.

"Am I wrong?"

"I don't know?"

Ugh. He wasn't helping. "Take your shirt off," I instructed.

He was caught off guard for some reason. "What? Why?"

I flexed my biceps as a reply.

"I'm good," he said anxiously. "We have to get ready."

And we did. Nothing too fancy. I just threw on a black and grey flannel and jeans. Fletcher wore one of my black polos and jeans as well. He was running hair wax in his black hair when I asked, "Why aren't you dating anyone?"

He shrugged his shoulders. "Not really interested in anyone."

"Liar," I accused. "Seriously dude, I've never seen you even try to hook up with any chick from our school. Or any other school as a matter of fact."

"Look what happened to Red," he said. He was referring to his three-girls-two-STDs-one-night incident. Was that his only reason? Fletcher was my boy and my best friend but he needed to get out in the dating world more.

I dropped the conversation and we started talking about something else. After we were done, we picked up Tristan then headed to Jason's. As we pulled into the parking lot, I noticed the place was already packed and the music was at full blast. Leave it to Jason to throw an epic party.

I had texted Trinity the address to the party earlier in the week. She said she was bringing some friends. Not that I really cared, we would probably be over by the end of the night. Once we were inside, I saw Jason with a cup already in his hand, saying something to some group of people. Ugh, this guy. Did he not learn the first time? I walked over and pulled the cup out of his hand.

Clemont was next to him. "It's only his first," he clarified.

"Yeah," I told him, "and probably his last. Where are the others?"

"Nolan is on his way and Red's outside somewhere."

I felt my phone vibrating. Trinity was calling and I hit the "ignore" option. I looked around to see if she was here but she wasn't in sight. Good. I needed a drink. I looked at Jason's cup in my hand. It was pretty full so I just started chugging it. It tasted like he mixed vodka with some Red Bull. After about an hour into the party, all my friends were trashed. As hard as I tried to keep Jason sober, he had a few drinks when I wasn't looking. Nolan arrived only to go straight to the alcohol. Clemont looked like he had the least to drink. Red was all over the place—quite the social butterfly he was. I sat on the couch between Fletcher and Tristan. Fletcher's bangs fell flat across his pale forehead. He always sweat when he drank. Tristan's freckles looked more pronounced when was intoxicated.

Tristan took a sip from his cup and stopped mid-drink to announce, "I'm gonna throw up," and got up and stumbled toward the bathroom. I was drinking, too. But at least I knew my limits. Pathetic Tristan.

"Lightweight," pointed out Fletcher. I agreed. "Hey, I think I see Trinity."

He pointed to a group of people and sure enough, he was right. Ugh, I didn't want to deal with her.

"Let's go to the roof, dude," I instructed, "before she sees me."

We made our way upstairs to Jason's bedroom. It was easier to climb out his window than it was to go to the backyard and climb up the side. Once we climbed out, we carefully made our way to the top and lay down. The sky was cloud free and full of stars. "How romantic," I said sarcastically.

"Right," agreed Fletcher. We heard the music on full blast from downstairs. I wondered how long it would be before Jason's neighbors called the cops to get him to turn it down. Not like it mattered, the cops practically knew Jason already. I felt my phone vibrate again. I pulled it out and saw Trinity calling again. Once I hit ignore, I got the "15 missed calls" notification. This chick was insane. Fletcher saw me ignore her call and snorted.

"What?" I chuckled.

"You're funny," he said. "Just leave her already."

"I want to," I pointed out. I really did, Trinity was too much to handle. She was hot as hell—don't get me wrong. But I didn't want to be tied down. I was way too young for that. I had my whole life to live.

"And you want me to be in a relationship… Why, again?"

"Know what? You're right, Fletcher. Stay single as long as you can."

He laughed while I pointed out every annoying detail about Trinity: her harassing phone calls, her annoying texts. I could go on for days. We made small talk about the game earlier and about graduation to pass the time. After a while, he was only giving me one-word or short answers. Something was bothering him. I had ways of making him talk.

"What's on your mind?"

"What do mean?" he asked.

"Come on, dude," I said. "You're drunk but you're not that drunk. Something's bothering you."

"It's nothing," he said. Why was he being complicated now? He just confirmed my suspicions that something was wrong. It wasn't like Fletcher to be upset. He was always the happiest out of everyone.

"Talk," I demanded.

He thought to himself for a while. He took a deep breath and turned to me. "We're best friends, right?"

I narrowed my eyes and wondered where he was going with this. "You know we are, dude."

"I just," he struggled. "I don't know…"

He trailed off. What was he getting at? Of course, we were best friends. Why wouldn't we be?

"You remember that time you got us all to try ecstasy?" he asked.

I chuckled. "Wasn't that an experience."

He gave me a light shove. "I still haven't forgiven you for that, you jerk. I don't think any of us have."

"Well, excuse me for trying to show my friends a good time. And a good time you all had, did you not?"

"Well, yeah…" he admitted, "but we all thought you had taken it, too."

I chuckled again. I remembered that night clearly. I had gotten a guy at school to hook me up with ecstasy. My friends and I were at one of Jason's parties and I said we would all try it together for the first time. I only pretended to take it while the others did. "You all seemed to be enjoying yourselves just fine."

"Fuck you, dude," he said with another shove. He was laughing now. Back then, all my friends were mad at the fact that they were rolling alone. It's whatever. It was thanks to me they had a good time.

"Or that time you got us to tag Atrisco High, 'member that?"

I chuckled again. "Hey, they started that fight. I just gave them what they had coming."

"We wouldn't have gotten caught either. Had it not been for Red dropping his phone at the scene."

"That dumb ass," I noted, "the media loved it, though. They started our own hashtag: '#TheSavageSeven.'" The vandalism we caused and the rivalry between the two schools spread across Albuquerque like wildfire. My

friends and I were on the front page of the newspaper several times. I could've written those articles better myself. But, it was free publicity in the end.

We were both laughing now. I've put my friends through a few crazy stunts. But, we all had fun no matter the consequences. Was this what Fletcher was trying to talk about? Past experiences? No, there had to be more.

"I'm glad we're friends, Zanniel" he said. "Like, for real, dude."

"No homo, though," I told him.

"Maybe a little homo."

"A little?" I turned to face him and next thing I knew, his lips were locked on mine. Was this really happening? Fletcher's eyes were closed but mine were wide open. Was this the alcohol talking? Or was he aware of what he was doing? I knew girls did this kind of thing when they would make out with each other and it'd be no big deal. But guys didn't do this, no way. I felt his jaw move as he started to make out with me rather than just plant a kiss. That wasn't even the scary part. What had me freaked even more *was the fact that I felt my jaw kissing him back. When I felt his tongue contact mine, that's when I pulled away.*

When Fletcher felt my lips leave his, his eyes shot open and he just stared at me. I stared back and neither of us said anything. What was *that? Fletcher was gay? I kissed him back. Did that make me gay? No. Hell no. I stood up and headed for Jason's window to go back downstairs.*

When I had gotten up, I froze at the sight of Tristan standing before me. Did he hear us? Did he see *us? He just stared at me. He looked pale and sick and I wondered how drunk he was. Before I knew it, vomit began gushing through his mouth and onto my shirt. What the* hell, *Tristan! I heard footsteps coming up behind me. I didn't want to look at Fletcher. I kept staring at Tristan long enough to realize I was counting the freckles on his cheeks.*

"You guys gay?" He asked in a flat tone. Shit. He did *see. I had to get down from here. I didn't even feel any type of intoxication in my body. I felt completely sober now as a matter of fact.*

I glanced over my shoulder to Fletcher. "Watch him," I instructed. I grabbed my flannel from the bottom and pulled up, careful not to touch Tristan's vomit. Once off, I just threw it on the roof. I needed water. I climbed down through the window and thought about grabbing one of Jason's shirts. His room was such a mess that I didn't know where to look. I decided to skip it and head downstairs topless.

Once downstairs, I looked around for my friends. Red was making out with some chick on the couch. Clemont was talking to a group of people I didn't recognize. I noticed he wasn't wearing his glasses. I headed to the kitchen and saw Jason talking to some blonde chick. He saw me and said something to the chick then headed my way.

He took note of my missing top. "Ummmm..." he tried.

"Tristan puked on me," I told him before he could find his words. He just started laughing. I felt a hand touch my shoulder. I turned around to see Nolan in front of me.

"Dude," he said, "where've you been? Trinity's going berserk looking for you."

I had completely forgotten about Trinity. I closed my eyes and tried to think. "Grab me a water," I told him. He was back in a flash with a bottled water in hand. He handed it to me and looked at me with curious eyes.

"Tristan puked on him," explained Jason before I could.

"Nice," replied Nolan. "Hey, have you seen Fletcher?"

I chugged the water fast and handed the empty bottle back to Nolan. "No," I lied. I looked around the groups of party people to see if I spotted Trinity anywhere. I began to feel claustrophobic and lightheaded. I stepped away from my friends without saying a word, heading outside. I needed air. Or solitude, one or the other. Once I stepped outside, I heard Trinity calling my name. I kept walking as I ignored her, but she ran to catch up to me.

"Zanniel!" She shrieked as she pulled my arm back.

I'd had it with her. "What? What, Trinity? What?!"

She looked startled at my angry tone. She didn't look like she'd been drinking. Her blonde hair was still done as well as her makeup. She did look hot tonight as she always did, but I couldn't take it anymore.

"I've been trying to call you," she said in a low voice.

"No shit." I turned away and she pulled me back around.

"Why aren't you wearing a shirt?"

"My friend puked all over me," I spat. I tried to turn around again but she pulled me back once more. Ugh! I yanked my arm free and glared at her.

"Why are you acting like this?"

"Because I'm done with this, Trinity."

She looked like she was on the verge of crying. "What did I do?"

"You annoy the shit out of me! You know that?"

You would've thought I slapped her by the way she looked at me. "Why? Because I really like you and I like talking to you?"

Ugh. I didn't want to have to be a dick to get her to back off. But if I didn't totally break her heart now, I was never going to get her off my back.

"There are no feelings here, Trinity. You are infatuated with this idea of us together. That's all. There's no us anymore. You got that? This was a mistake, you were a mistake. Now do me a favor and leave me the hell alone."

I heard her starting to sob. "Can't we talk about it?"

Was she seriously asking me that? Why would she want to keep this going after everything I'd just said? Why would she be willing to try and work on something that I've made clear was a mistake? I didn't get it. I placed my hands on her shoulders and looked her straight in the eyes. "Listen to me. There's nothing to talk about. I don't want you, Trinity. Don't call me, don't text me. Pretend I don't exist. Do I make myself clear?"

She was taking deep breaths to keep from crying, but tears were falling down her cheeks. "But I was a virgin when I met you!"

"Yeah," I agreed, "I could tell." That last comment on my part was unnecessary, I know. Oh, well. I don't need her in my life, and this is how I was going to make that happen. She started letting out loud sobs. She turned

around and ran back inside the house. I pulled my keys out of my pocket and headed for my Suburban. I wasn't ready to leave yet—I just wanted to be alone.

Once I got in my car, I just reclined the seat back and started thinking. No more Trinity, awesome. Fletcher kissed me, not awesome. What did this mean? Was my best friend gay? Not that it mattered if he was or not. But I kissed him back! What did that make me? I wasn't into guys. Then again, I just dumped a really hot chick… I was starting to regret that now. Should I call her? Apologize? I knew she'd take me back in a heartbeat. But did I really want that? Ugh! I punched the steering wheel out of frustration.

I searched my pockets for my phone but had no luck. I probably left it on the roof somewhere. "Ugh!!!" I grunted. This party was shit. No, this whole night *was shit. What else could go wrong? Then I thought to myself, nothing. I took deep breaths. Nothing is wrong. Everything is fine. I took more deep breaths to try calm myself down.*

After a few breathing exercises, I was better. I got out of my vehicle and headed back to the party. Nothing is wrong and nothing will go wrong. Once inside, I made my way upstairs to Jason's room. I passed some guy pouring shots in small glasses. I reached for one as I walked and gulped it down. Feeling the alcohol burn in my throat gave me a reminder that this was a party. I should be having fun. *Once I got to Jason's room, I threw on the first shirt I saw. "Raven Athletics" read the black shirt. Whether it was clean or dirty was beyond me, I just put it on. I then headed for the window and climbed up to the roof.*

I made my way over to where Fletcher and I were sitting, but there was no sign of my phone or Fletcher anywhere. Ugh! I looked all around without any success. I even walked dangerously to the edge to see if it had slid down. Nope, nothing.

"Looking for this?"

I whipped my head around and saw Fletcher on the other side of the roof. There was a bright light on his hand that I could only assume was my phone.

I took a deep breath and walked over to him. He handed my phone over and I mumbled, "Thanks."

"I thought Red was the one who dropped his phone everywhere?" He was talking to me so casually. Did he not remember what he just did? Or was he just going to pretend like it never happened? If he wasn't bringing it up, I wasn't either.

Play it cool, Zanniel. "Right."

"I see you found a shirt?"

"Yeah," I agreed, "one of Jason's."

"Nice. Hey, I couldn't help but overhear what went down with Trinity."

That threw me off. I was almost sure he was going bring up the kiss. Did he really hear us talk from all the way up here? I kept reminding myself to keep cool. "Yeah, it's whatever. It was bound to happen."

He shrugged his shoulders. So that was it? Were we never speaking of this again? What about Tristan? He saw us kiss. Where was he? "Hey, where'd Tristan go?"

"I got him down and he crashed out on Jason's bed. Didn't you see him when you came up?"

"Must've missed him." So that was the end of it? It must be. Fletcher wasn't gay and neither was I. The more I talked to him, the more I convinced myself that it never even happened. I thought for a while as I stared at my phone. Fletcher must've said something but I'd completely spaced 'cause I heard him say, "Earth to Zanniel?"

"What?" I was lost. Fletcher laughed. He was acting so normal that I looked like the one who was off.

"You alright, bro?" I had to stop. I was acting weird. I know I was. Nothing is wrong. I just had to keep telling myself that.

"A little drunk, maybe?" We both laughed and headed back down to join the others. The party wasn't in full blast when we got downstairs. People weren't drinking, dancing, laughing, making out; our typical Jason-type party was at a pause. The cops had showed up to tell us to turn the music down. They hardly ever showed up anymore. We did as we were told only

to turn it back up as soon as they left. No one was stopping our party. I felt better, too. Once I stopped thinking about Fletcher's kiss, the night returned to normal and we partied till around two in the morning.

Fletcher and I decided to crash at Jason's. There was no way I could drive home as inebriated as I was. Jason didn't mind. He had a huge house with three different guest rooms. I don't know where his parents were—they were never around. He was also an only child, so I could relate to him when the feelings of abandonment came from not having parents around. He also had a maid that was probably not looking forward to cleaning up the disaster left behind.

My friends decided to stay, too. Nolan stayed in one room, Red in the other with some chick, and Clemont took up the third. Jason crashed on the couch, seeing as how Tristan was passed out on his bed. The only bedroom left was his parents. I wasn't sure if we were allowed in there, but I was too drunk to care.

When we got to the top of the stairs and to his parents' bedroom, Fletcher let himself in first and stumbled on something falling to the floor. What a drunk, I thought to myself. I laughed at his stupidity and clumsiness. I went over to help him up but when I stretched out my arm to help him up he pulled me down to him. He fell on purpose!

I fell on top of him. He was looking deep into my eyes with a grin on his face. I felt a little uncomfortable but I didn't move. I swallowed a big gulp that had formed in my throat and just as I was about to say something, he leaned up and locked his lips to mine. Again. I pulled back this time. He started to breathe heavily. Not sure if it was the situation making him nervous or if it was the weight of my body crushing him. He looked paler than usual and I hoped he wasn't about to throw up. I found myself moving his black bangs from his eyes with my hand. His black eyes. In a way they were alluring, almost captivating.

Without thinking, I leaned down and kissed him back. The thought was disgusting and I knew I should pull away. But I didn't. I felt his jaw move and I was lost in the moment. Stop! I told myself. Fletcher stared to kiss harder—it kind of hurt my lips a little. I could taste alcohol on his tongue and wondered what all of this was. Were we just two drunk teens letting our testosterone get the better of us? Or was there more? More beyond the boundaries of our friendship that I was completely blind to up until this point? I didn't know.

Fletcher pulled off my shirt and began to undo my pants. Were we really doing this? How did this work? I'm not a virgin but I've only slept with girls. I was not sure how this was going to happen seeing as Fletcher had different body parts. Fletcher took his shirt off—well, it was my *shirt he wore—and I decided to not think anymore. I let my pants come off and gave into the moment.*

I felt Fletcher taking his pants off and realized both our man parts were equally stiff. Did I really want to do this? Why? Never before tonight had I ever felt an excitement like this toward another guy. That's just wrong. Or was it? I turned my brain off then and decided to just give myself to Fletcher. I wasn't sure what was going to happen after tonight but that didn't matter. Not right now at least.

XI

Distortion

Lennox was no expert about Limbo. She was just as lost as the rest of us. Why would she think Clyde wasn't dead? After he vanished for a few seconds and didn't appear again, I thought he was gone for good. But electric currents moved around the spot where he was lying, and sure enough he was back. His strange episode seemed to have ended after a few more cycles. He sat up and looked at us. He was sweating and taking deep breaths.

"Clyde," asked Lennox as she stepped closer to him, "what just happened.?"

Clyde didn't respond right away. He looked confused. "A room."

"Room?" pressed Lennox. "Room. What room?"

I rolled my eyes. She could at least let the guy process things on his own before trying to explain to us. Part of me hoped that she would drop the whole Trinity-connection. Looking back at that eventful night, there are several things I would've done differently. But it was the *past*. Why was she so upset over it? Even Trinity accepted the break up and left me alone afterwards.

Clyde sighed. "Ah dunno."

Lennox tucked her blonde locks behind her ears and squatted close to him. "What do you remember?"

He shook his head and closed his eyes. "Ah dunno."

"This room, what was in it?"

"D'you not jus' hear me?" It was hilarious seeing others talk back to Lennox in ways she wasn't expecting. I think all of us here have at least snapped at her once for her constant nagging.

She kept trying. "I did. But I just want to know—"

"Why?" he interrupted. I don't think he meant to sound like a jerk. If anything, he was probably frustrated trying to figure things out *himself.* Explaining what you don't know sounds like a headache. He already told her twice that he didn't know. But, what I've learned from Lennox—she can be pushy, reminded me a lot of Trinity.

"Okay," she breathed as she stood up, "talk to us when you're ready."

She sounded too calm. I know it was eating at her, but she played it off cool. I wondered myself what Clyde had seen. Where did he go? Why did he go there? Lennox turned back around and began stomping her red heels toward me. Her face looked hard, determined. "Back to *you.*"

I grunted in frustration. "You want me to apologize or something?"

She stopped directly in front of me. "It's too late for that. Did you ever think about consequences, Zanniel? Did you ever stop and think how the things you did would affect everyone around you?"

"No," I told her. I really didn't. Why should I preoccupy my mind with what would happen to others? That's irrelevant to me and a waste of time. Everyone needs to look out for themselves. Why was she lecturing? Ugh, and I thought *Trinity* was annoying—Lennox surpassed that effortlessly.

"Of course not. If you did, I wouldn't be dead. My life would be just as perfect as it used to be *before* you stepped in the picture."

"Back off, *mother,*" I hissed. "I don't need lectures right now from anyone, especially *you!*"

"That's an allegation," noted Tristan. "What proof do you have that Zanniel did anything to you?"

Tristan was right. But, Lennox looked determined to prove that this was more than just an allegation. She was even shaking her head at Tristan as he spoke. "You don't have to stick up for him every chance you get."

"You don't have to speak every chance you get, either. But you still do." As funny as Tristan's counter-remark was, I didn't laugh. Lennox had me suddenly intrigued with her allegation. Now I wanted to know why she believed what she did.

"Tell me," I said, "how did I mess up your 'perfect life'?"

As I put up air quotes, I heard Clyde scoff. "Y'all are jus' a couple a dicks ain't ya?"

I heard him but I ignored him. Now he wants to talk? Whatever. My attention was on Lennox. I crossed my arms over my chest and stared at her. "I'm waiting?"

She looked around at the others as if to get some sort of reassurance. Clyde still sat on the ground. Satchel was pacing around us not contributing to the argument, thankfully. She took a deep breath and closed her eyes. Talk about dramatic.

"Do you know what a chain reaction is?"

My typical answer to that would be "a reaction of chains." But I held back on that instead. "Yes, Lennox. I know what that is."

"Well, you started one, the night you broke up with Trinity."

I decided to keep quiet and just listen to her. Tristan opened his mouth to say something but I put up my hand in front of his face. He closed his mouth and knew to stay quiet. I just stared at Lennox, trying my best to keep a straight face. She didn't need to know when or why her words had an impact on me.

"Trinity cheered at Cueva with me. You probably already knew that. Well, not only was she one of my best friends, but she was main base in my stunt group, and I was a flyer. And a good flyer I was."

She began moving around in place as she spoke. She turned to the side and bent her left leg as if she was doing a quad stretch. Then she grabbed her toe with her left hand, pulled it up behind her, and grabbed it with her right. A scorpion, I thought to myself. I helped Trinity stretch a few times so I somehow learned the proper names of the skills. Lennox was more flexible than Trinity was, though.

I also noticed she was wearing black spandex-like shorts under her red skirt. *Another* thing that Trinity did as well. They were like me in a way: I would always wear gym shorts under all my pants. Guess cheerleaders did the same, only with spandex instead.

"We had our state cheer competition one month after your basketball win against us," she continued, "as perfect as our routine was, not every cheerleader was in the right state of mind.

"Trinity was distraught after you left her." She put her leg down. "She was always crying, distracted, a complete mess. Well, if you know anything about cheer and stunting, we all must work together to make our stunts hit. If someone isn't in the right place at the right time with the right grip, that's when stunting gets *very* dangerous."

She turned to face us head on. She kicked up her left leg in front of her, above her head, and caught her heel with both hands. She kept her leg straight as she pulled her left arm in front of her left leg, causing her leg to turn to the side. A bow and arrow, I thought to myself. Talk about flexible. She could kiss her knee if she wanted to. Why was she showing off? "Needless to say," she continued as she put her leg down, "on the day of our competition, Trinity was still just as shattered. Our friend, who was also my side base, Destiny, was also in a strange funk. She was throwing up all morning. I did my best to calm them both down, seeing as this was the most important day of our entire season. But, my efforts were ineffective.

"During warm up, we did okay. A few stunts were a little shaky but I had faith in my team. I kept trying to throw good vibes left and right with the hopes that we could deliver a solid performance and keep our state title from past years. But good vibes weren't enough." She crossed her arms over her chest. "Surprisingly, we were doing better than we did during warm-up when we actually began our performance in front of the judges. Or cheer section went great. All stunts hit and the crowd was pumped. When our music started playing, we started our tumble passes. I threw mine, but Trinity and Destiny didn't. Not that it made a difference in our choreography 'cause they made it to their spots for our jump section right on time."

As she was telling us her story, she would stare blindly and have awkward pauses. Like she was reliving the moment in her head. She also spoke as if talking to herself rather than to us. "After jumps, we went on to our dance. After a few eight-counts there, it was time for our pyramid. We did some braced inversions and complicated transitions. When we were down to our last eight-count, the last pose…that's when my nightmare began."

She whispered the last part. She spun in a circle in place, turning over her right shoulder. She hit a V motion with her arms extended when she turned back to us. "As simple as a full-up stunt like that was, my bases weren't focused. As I went up and spun, Trinity didn't have the correct grip, and as much as I tried to be tight and fight for the stunt, I failed. Destiny couldn't catch my foot to provide the platform I needed to stay in the air. Instead, I found myself continuing to turn and falling backwards. All the spotters were behind our stunt group so they didn't catch me as I fell forward.

"I remember landing on my back and squirming in pain. We were stunting on mats so they absorbed some of the impact. I don't remember passing out, but I woke up in the hospital. I was so confused, but Trinity and Destiny were there and they filled me in on what happened. Trinity blamed herself for the accident, said it was her fault for not paying attention. Destiny said she was just as guilty for throwing up all day and being sick. I heard what they had to say but I didn't blame them one bit. Life happens and it just gets in the way sometimes.

"At the hospital, I got diagnosed with spondylosis. It's every cheerleader's worst fear: being told they can never cheer again. Yes, it was my senior year but I was still looking forward to cheerleading in college.

I thought maybe I'd even get a chance to join Team USA and represent in the world championship. Maybe even all-stars. But, no."

I've heard of spondylosis before. Lennox basically tore her spine. Why was she so upset? It was just cheerleading. Cheerleaders at Rio fell on their faces a lot and they still managed to keep going. "You still could've cheered if you wanted," I pointed out. "It'd just hurt like hell."

"*Thanks,*" she mocked, "it wasn't that simple. The pain was too unbearable. A simple back handspring made it feel like someone stabbed me with a knife." She bent her knees slightly then jumped backwards into a said back handspring. She probably couldn't do that when she was alive but she performed the skill effortlessly. And in *heels* nonetheless. When she landed on her feet, she smoothed her blonde hair back and breathed out into a smile.

Before Trinity, I dated a chick at Rio who talked about cheerleading the way Trinity and Lennox did. Her name was Jauni. She was a ten all around but she was always busy with cheer. Couldn't hang after school 'cause she had practice. She couldn't hang at night 'cause she would cheer games on the sidelines while I was on the team playing. She couldn't meet up for breakfast 'cause they had morning practices. Even weekends were a hassle; she had tumbling classes to go to. Granted, she *was* captain so she had more responsibilities than a regular team member did. But I never saw the point of all the hard work she put into it. The stunting was cool to watch but all they did was yell our mascot, school colors, and spell our school's name over and over. I always argued with Trinity *and* Jauni on how cheerleading wasn't considered a sport. There was no way that waving pom-poms, dancing, and doing a few flips and stunts was considered a sport. But, these girls were stubborn and by the sound of Lennox's history, she would argue just the same.

"That was only the beginning," she continued. "I was hoping to get a cheerleading scholarship had I made the university team. Destiny and Trinity made it but I didn't even make the first cut. My parents wouldn't pay for school unless I went into the medical field. I wanted to go for cosmetology and they didn't approve. Trinity was going for nursing and Destiny for pharmacy and as much as I wanted to follow their examples, I just couldn't. I applied for a few scholarships and loans but that didn't get me far; school was too expensive. It was pretty depressing watching my best friends follow their dreams: cheering for the university, having their school paid for, and they even joined a sorority. Our little trio became a duo."

Was her sob-story relevant? So, she couldn't cheer again. *Big deal.* So, according to Lennox, Trinity technically caused her injury because of me? No. That to me is just looking for someone to blame. Shit happens, we deal with it, then we move on. Now that she got that out of the way, was she going to tell us how she died? That's what I really wanted to know. I still remember her talking about a "he" when I first encountered her. "He" who? I wanted to ask her to get to the point already. Tristan must've read my thoughts 'cause he beat me to the punch. "So how did you die?"

Lennox threw him a look as if to say, "Really?" Tristan mimicked her facial expression back at her. "I got thrown from the roof of a five-story hotel," she told him.

Oh, *shit.* That wasn't what I was expecting to hear. I remembered back to downtown when I first saw her lifeless body on the ground. Her body *had* been in a weird position. It makes sense if that's what she looked like when she hit the ground. But why? What could she have done to get thrown overboard? Her whole life turned to shit, basically. Who'd she piss off?

"That's brutal," said Tristan. "Who threw you?"

"Oh, I'm sorry," she said sarcastically. "If you would've waited and not interrupted me, I would've gotten to that part."

They glared at each other. Had we all still been alive, I can't help but think that these two would somehow be together. They already bickered back and forth like a married couple. It was hilarious to watch. I wondered how Jason had put up with her.

"Anyways," she continued, "where was I…?"

"Trinity 'n' Destiny," piped in Clyde. Everyone was caught off guard, he'd been so quiet all this time. He hadn't got up. He remained seated and looked up at Lennox. Satchel was leaning against a tree a few feet away, but close enough to hear.

"Right," managed Lennox after an awkward pause, "thank you."

"Sure," he replied and then she continued.

"My friends did their best to include me in everything they did, but it didn't help that they were living the lives I wanted so badly. After a while, I began to distance myself. Eventually, Destiny got engaged to a guy she'd been dating for a while. Instead of the traditional wedding, all she wanted was a few days away with her soon-to-be-husband in Vegas. On the night of her bachelorette party, we all went to a strip club. Some place called 'Fantasy' something. It just so happened to be amateur night when we were there, so any girl in the crowd could go up on stage and give a show."

A strip club? Nice. Lennox didn't come off as the type of chick that would ever step into such a place. Then again, she was wearing these hooker-heels and a really short skirt. I questioned whether or not she was wearing a bra under her top. I couldn't really tell 'cause of the jacket. Either way, she had me hooked. What did she do at this place?

"Destiny and Trinity both went up on stage and gave a show. Nothing too big, just a few hip movements and they failed miserably at trying to use the pole. Destiny got thirty in tips and Trinity got twenty. Then, they both insisted I *live* a little and give it a try. I was resisting at first but I gave into pressure. I was wearing a halter dress, sort of like this one, only longer. My friends said I wasn't going to get any tips with it on. They stripped me from it in a matter of seconds. Thankfully I had a sports bra and spandex shorts underneath. The rhinestone heels and bow I had on made me look a little whore-ish, but I didn't have a say.

"Once they threw me on stage, I was in complete panic. I heard a song come on and recognized it immediately. It was the one song 'Up in the Air' by Thirty Seconds to Mars. Being on stage and having all eyes on me reminded me a lot of performing a cheer routine. Once I compared the feeling, all panic was gone. As soon as the vocals dropped, I began swaying my hips, moving my arms around my body… I became alive.

"I tried one swing at the pole and regretted it almost immediately. I stopped mid-swing and placed my hand over my lower back. I froze for a moment trying to recover from the pain. But, then I started doing cheer-stretch poses and the crowd went wild. Their favorite was—"

She touched the ground with both hands and slowly slid into the middle splits. Damn. I'll admit, that was both hot and seductive. I can see how and why that was the crowd favorite.

"When the song was over and I collected tips," she continued, but stayed in the same position, "I counted seventy-five. I didn't think I was *that* good. But the generosity proved otherwise. When my friends and I were getting ready to leave, someone grabbed my arm. When I turned, I didn't recognize the stranger before me. He had slicked back hair and wore a suit without an under shirt. A pimp, I thought. He said he wanted to hand me my tip personally. So, he slid a hundred-dollar bill into my hand. I thought he was crazy, but he insisted I take it. Then he asked for a private dance to the same song…"

She trailed off. She stared blankly in front of her as if she was replaying that night in her head. A hundred-dollar tip? Was she *that* good? Or did this pimp just have more than enough bills to hand out? I stared at her as she thought to herself.

"And?" My voice brought her back.

"And I was desperate for money. So, I went to the private room with him. I didn't know what I was doing. I just mimicked what I saw the strippers at the club do. What started off as a lap dance turned into some weird sexual thrill for him. One moment he was on the chair, the next he had me pressed up against the wall inhaling my scent. He kept grinding his body on mine and snapping his teeth at me. He would moan and groan to himself and all I wanted was for the song to end so I could get out of there. I didn't feel him slip any bills in my bra or shorts. But, he did. When the song finally ended, I got out as fast as I could and went straight to the bathroom. I kept taking deep breaths and fanning myself to keep from crying. When I pulled out all the bills he had placed on me, I counted up to $1,200."

Tristan scoffed. "That's exaggerating. $1,200 from one dance?"

"It's not exaggerating," she clarified, "I couldn't believe it myself."

Her story was taking too long. "Okay, so you had a little girls' night out at a strip club. Congratulations. How does that explain your death?" Why couldn't she just get to the point? I saw her smile faintly as she moved her legs back in to get up.

She stood up and put her hands on her hips. "That night started my little hobby. No cheerleading, no scholarships, no money, no *life*. I needed to change all that. But I needed to do it in a way I only knew how: with my looks. As conceited as that sounds, I got over a grand at a strip club by doing an amateur dance. I could only imagine the persuasion I could achieve with other wealthy pervs. But I didn't want to become a stripper, or a prostitute at that. Not that I'm proud, but I became sort of a cat."

"*What?*" I responded, "you started robbing people?" I did *not* see that one coming. I knew Lennox had looks but to connivingly use them to get what she wanted? Talk about deceptive.

She shook her head. "I know it sounds horrible, and believe me, I am not proud. But, I was just trying to survive. That's no excuse and I sound awful for trying to justify my actions. I was desperate."

"That's an understatement," pointed out Tristan, "how did you even pull that off?"

Lennox took a deep breath. "I never did these things in Albuquerque, it was too risky. I went out of my way to make sure I was far from home. I went to places like Belen, Hobbs, Roswell, Cruces, and even Carlsbad. I went to bars and strip clubs looking quite seductive and to be honest, a little trashy. I would put on temporary dye in my hair, wear sunglasses, and anything to change my appearance completely.

"Once I got the attention of a complete stranger. I would let them sweet talk me, buy me a drink. Then after a few minutes of idle chit chat, they would take me away. Sometimes a hotel, sometimes their homes… but, I always made sure to slip a few roofies, either before or after we got there. Once they got knocked out, I would wipe them clean. Wallets, jewelry, anything of value really."

What?! Damn, talk about date rape. No wonder Lennox wasn't in heaven. There were countless ways for her to get money and survive. Why did she settle for this? Not only was it wrong to leave a guy with blue balls like that, thinking that they were going to get lucky. But, talk about playing with fire. Was the "he" she mentioned earlier one of the guys she robbed? I thought back to Satchel and my friends and how they came for me as a group. Did they come for her like that as well?

"That went on for a while," she continued. "Shameless indeed, but I actually enjoyed myself. I knew that eventually I would get stopped. But I never imagined it would go the way it did." Her facial expression changed. She looked sad now, worried. Maybe remorseful?

"I made the mistake the mistake of getting picked up by a detective," she said more slowly, "a detective that apparently had been on my trail from a few past theft reports. I was so naïve when I got to the motel with him. I thought he was just another pervert looking for a good time. I had handcuffed him to the bed with one arm. When I was going to handcuff the other, he pulls out a badge and says I'm being placed under arrest. I thought he was joking at first. But, he started mentioning places I'd been and I panicked. He hadn't consumed my tampered drink like I thought he had. He started shouting some very menacing things when he saw I was making my getaway. He even pulled out his gun and fired a few rounds in my direction. I don't know how but I managed to snatch his car keys before I stormed out of there. Once I got in his car, I drove all the way back to Albuquerque and left him restrained to a bed somewhere in Belen.

"I left his car somewhere off the side of the road and got a taxi to a nearby restaurant. I don't remember where I went or what I ordered, but I just remember crying my eyes out. I was scared to death. That same night at that same restaurant, Jason noticed me sitting alone and looking a hot mess. He came to comfort me with the whole 'Don't I know you' approach. He sat with me and we began talking. Strangely enough, he had a way of making me feel better. After that night, he and I were inseparable. He eventually popped the question about two months before I was killed."

Why did Jason never mention Lennox to me? They didn't date very long. But, you would think I would've seen her *somewhere* in at least a picture or something. Nothing. Or maybe I missed it? I was busy myself with my fraternity, basketball, and life at the university all together; was I just too busy to notice?

"I have no idea how that detective even found me months later. I was at my rehearsal dinner when I saw him in the crowd of guests. I thought I was hallucinating. He was sitting with my friend Destiny and I don't see how she would even know him. I had to get air. I needed to clear my mind. I went to the higher floor, out to the roof and felt the nightly breeze. I heard someone come up behind me, and at that moment, I knew I wasn't wrong—I had seen correctly. 'Look what the cat dragged in,' he taunted. After a few more remarks like that, he soon had me cornered. I tried getting away but he got physical. Grabbed me and threw me around the roof. I begged him to stop but he was enjoying my misery. He was more furious at the fact that I had gotten away and made him look like a fool rather than the actual crime he was trying to charge me with. He made that clear a few times. Said I took his manhood from him and he was going to get it back one way or another.

"He picked me up by neck and before he threw me over the ledge, he told me, 'I asked you once if it hurt when you fell from heaven. Let me know if it hurts falling from here.' And before I knew it, I was falling. All the way down…"

She got quiet then. Looks like that guy got his revenge. But what was Lennox thinking? She knew that everything she was doing was wrong. It was bound to catch up to her eventually. It's funny how Jason played a part in all of this. She said they'd been inseparable ever since but what if Jason hadn't been there? Would she still be doing all these crazy stunts? Would she still be dead?

"You mean Destiny Miller?" asked Clyde. We all turned to him. He was still on the ground. He was referring to the Destiny that Lennox had mentioned, her friend. Did he know her? "Better yet, once known as 'Destiny Archibeque'?"

Lennox looked stunned. She opened her mouth to respond but no words came out. She and Clyde just stared at each other. Clyde lifted his left hand revealing a wedding band on his on his finger I hadn't noticed before. "*My* Destiny?" Was the Destiny in Lennox's story the same as Clyde's apparent wife? She must be. But how could Lennox not have seen Clyde before, then? Same question I ask as to why she never saw me when I dated Trinity? Were guys simply not mentioned or seen inside their little friendship circle?

"Oh, my god," breathed Lennox. "How could that be?"

Just then, I got a whiff of smoke. Like something was burning. Not only that, there was a change to the sky: it got darker and I wasn't mistaken, the air and clouds were beginning to circulate around us again. Something off the side got Lennox's attention. She let out a scream and covered her mouth. I turned to see what she saw. It was Satchel. He was standing in place with his hands and head shaking frantically. It wasn't the fact that his eyes had rolled to the back of his head that had me in sudden fear, it was the fact that there were flames emanating from the ground beneath him.

XII

Burning

Since I gave into the Lennox's Limbo theory and we started talking about heaven and hell, I couldn't help but wonder exactly *where* I would end up going. Once I saw that Satchel was here as well and after hearing his insane explanation of his psychopathic conversion, I was sure he belonged in hell. I didn't know exactly how things worked, but I was pretty sure that murdering numerous people while on a mission of revenge didn't exactly save you a seat in heaven. That sounded more like a one-way ticket to hell. It looked like right before my eyes, that very thing was taking place.

Clyde instantly jumped to his feet and stepped away from Satchel with the rest of us. The wind picked up faster around us and it looked like the dark clouds in the dark sky were in motion. Satchel kept shaking all around. The flames beneath his feet were building. Was he feeling the flames? He wasn't making sounds or giving any indication that he was in pain, even though he looked just that. What do we do? Just watch? Was this the last time we were going to see Satchel?

The ground began shaking and even began to part in a few places. Through the cracks, a faint red glow as well as more flames were in view. Satchel dropped to his knees and looked to be heaving. He tilted his head back and let out a scream up to the sky. There was an edge to his voice. Agony? Pain? He must've been feeling *something* terrible to have let out a sound like that.

He shifted his weight forward onto his hands. The ground beneath him looked to be giving in, like he was sinking into the earth. The flames grew more pronounced so that his whole body was now covered in fire. I couldn't look away. I wanted to see the faces of the others, but I felt frozen in place. I heard thunder rumbling and soon after saw lightning. Not in the sky, but fading in and out with the foggy wind currents that were swirling around us.

After a few moments of just staring at Satchel's combustion, a flash appeared where he was. Not like Axel's bright light, but more of a faint flare. Before I knew it, he was gone. As I stared in shock at the pile of dirt and ash that remained. Somehow, it started to rain. Slow drops at first, then it began to pour. The winds around us slowed down, and all that we were left with of Satchel was the mere memory of him.

It was silent now except for the splashing of the rain drops. I turned to the others and saw that Lennox was holding on to Tristan. How *romantic*. Clyde just stared straight ahead. And then there were four of us. First Axel, now Satchel. Who was next? And how is the order even determined? I turned to Lennox and broke the silence. "So, what now, date rape? Is that what's in store for the rest of us?"

She turned to me, but still held on to Tristan. She shook her head. "I don't know." Her voice was breaking. "I don't know, Zanniel. Okay?"

"Great," I said with disappointment. "When I actually need you, you become *useless*."

"Hey," defended Tristan, "that's counterproductive."

Was he serious? He was *defending* her? Just moments ago, he couldn't even stand her! Talk about hypocrisy. I wonder if Lennox was freaked now because what happened to Satchel could potentially be her fate as well. She was no saint after all.

"We ain't done puttin' pieces together," piped in Clyde. I knew he was right. Clearly, we were all connected in way or another. Everyone had had a chance to speak of the things they've done. Well, except

Tristan. But, Clyde had more connection to this than just marriage to this Destiny character. What was he not telling us?

"Well said, officer," I remarked. "So go. Put *your* pieces in place."

He didn't respond. He just stared at me with his blue eyes. He was giving me that stern menacing look cops gave you when they wanted you to talk. But it was the opposite here. *He* had talking to do.

Rain continued to pour. We all were completely wet, but I didn't feel any of the rain drops on me. My clothes were soaked, but I didn't feel a difference from when they were dry. I stared at Clyde with the same look he was giving me. What, was he not going to disclose any of his past?

"Lennox," I summoned, without tearing my gaze away, "you're annoyingly persuasive; get at him."

She probably rolled her eyes at me or something. Before she could talk, Clyde spoke up. "Ah wanted the better-most for Destiny." Okay?

"She went for nothing but hooligans," he continued. "Ah made sure I'd be different. Made sure she was 'appy as can be!"

"Cut to the chase," I told him. "What did you do?" I didn't need him to start telling us a full biography of his life the way Lennox did. It was hard enough to understand his southern accent. I didn't feel like hearing more than I had to.

"Ah made sure she had 'erself a miscarriage."

"*What?*" Asked Lennox. Why was she so surprised? After seeing Axel go to heaven, Satchel to hell, and whatever Clyde had gone through, you would think she was used to such surprises by now. But, no. Everything still fazed her apparently. "Destiny was pregnant?"

"Sure was."

"When? How?" She shook her head and let go of Tristan. Some friends *she* had. Not only did they not meet the guys their friends dated, but they kept things from each other, too. Reminds me a little of my friends. Anyways, causing a miscarriage? That was technically murder on his part if *he* was the reason it happened.

"She 'ad 'er whole life t' live," he answered. "Ah sure wasn' 'bout to take it from 'er."

Clyde looked like he was about to cry. It could be the wetness on his face from the rain, or he could genuinely be sorry for what he did. Funny to see a guy as big as Clyde looking so small. Talk about pathetic. More importantly, how did he cause a miscarriage? Lennox was just as interested in learning about this whole situation since it involved her friend, so I left questioning up to her. "When was she pregnant?"

"Day of yer lil competition. All the throwin' up she was doin'? Yeah, mornin' sickness."

"If she was pregnant, why was she performing?" Lennox sounded like she was lecturing Clyde. In a way, I guess she was.

"She didn' know."

Lennox shook her head. "Then, how did *you?*"

Clyde closed his eyes and pinched the bridge of his nose. "We wen' fer a checkup an' her results said she wasn' pregnan'. But clinic folks got 'er tests mixed up with 'nother gal's."

Lennox crossed her arms over her chest. "And how did *you* get the news instead of Destiny?"

"Had 'er phone. Got a call from a number she didn' 'ave saved."

"So, you answered it," she accused. She was being really hostile toward Clyde now. "What gave you the right? Just because you were the father?"

"She wasn' ready!" He looked furious. Lennox probably hit a nerve. "You think Ah like carryin' this damn secret?! Knowin' Ah killed our 'nborn child?!"

It was obvious that Clyde felt guilty for what he did. I can understand where he was coming from. Why would he force Destiny to have a child that she wasn't ready for? Why throw away her future by forcing the responsibility of being a parent on her? The child wasn't even born yet, so he didn't technically kill it. It's wrong, yes. But understandable. I'm siding with Clyde on this one.

"How could you do that to her?" She asked. She looked disgusted. Then she gasped and looked like she just realized something. "So, if that's the reason she was feeling sick during competition, you could've stopped it! You could've prevented her from performing and kept me from hitting the ground!"

Lennox was very good at jumping to conclusions. The fact that her friend was pregnant and was a partial cause of her injury was probably just a coincidence. Lennox is just looking to make the pieces fit. Blaming others seemed to happen a lot here in Limbo.

Lennox walked away from us. How dramatic. Like really, where was she going to go? I was half-expecting Tristan to go after her, but he just turned to me and shrugged his shoulders. I didn't have anything to contribute to Clyde's story, seeing as it didn't involve me.

Or did it? "When did you meet Destiny, anyway?" I asked.

My question turned his attention toward me. He chuckled. Not in a funny way, more of a I-can't-believe-this kind of way. Only, what was he getting at? He didn't immediately answer my question. He thought for a few moments first.

"Same party you were at."

What?! Curveball again! How was that possible? No, there was no way. Tristan turned to me with his brow furrowed. "That's far-fetched. Why would you even think that?"

"Ah 'ave ears. Been listening to you folks chitchat and put everythin' 'gether. Party after a game of Rio vs Cueva. Destiny was a cheerleader on the same team as Lennox here. 'Er friend Trinity jus' got heartbroken by some asshole.

"Ah was jus' startin' off as a cadet. Did a ride alon' to a party makin' too much noise. Ah get there in time to see 'er leavin'. A lil small talk an' she 'ad me hooked. Got 'er number that night an' we were hand 'n' glove after that."

No. No, no, no, no, no, no. No! That party couldn't have been *that* eventful. Not only was that party the day Fletcher showed me how he really felt. But, Lennox met Jason, Clyde met Destiny, got her pregnant, and she along with broken-hearted Trinity cause Lennox to break her back. I didn't say anything, but I knew I had a look on my face that made me look shocked. Maybe even scared?

I heard Lennox's heels coming back this way. No doubt she must've figured out the same thing I did. Well, besides Fletcher's kiss. Everything else fit perfectly. Perfectly in some strange, twisted, fateful way. I didn't have to turn to her to know she was about to come at me with the accusations again.

"Why am I not surprised that this has something to do with *you*," she barked. "So basically, my accident at state was not only caused by you breaking Trinity's heart but inviting her, Destiny and me to a party where Clyde would meet Destiny, knocking her up? Causing both of my bases to be out of sync with the rest of the team, making my stunt fail?"

I didn't answer her. She made her way back toward us but stopped inches from my face. The rain had slowed down to a drizzle and the moving fog in the air had came to a halt. Lennox didn't blink as she stared into my eyes. Such hate she probably had toward me. Oh, well. Her problem, not mine. I stood my ground. "Are you done barking?"

Before I had time to react, she raised her right hand and smacked me across the face. I didn't feel her blow, but I heard a loud *smack*. I slowly turned back to her and saw that she was crying. Why was she so upset with *me*? It was not my fault Trinity didn't know how to handle a breakup nor was it my fault that Destiny didn't know how to use a condom.

"Who was he?" Asked Clyde. Lennox turned to him but didn't answer. "This detective ah yours, who was he?"

She opened her mouth and then closed it. She looked thrown off by his sudden interest. But she'd just slapped me. I *had* to say something. "Does it really matter, officer? She's already *dead* after all." Was he trying to get a description of him? Normally that happens when cops are trying to find a suspect. But we're in *Limbo*. I doubt he's going to find any suspects here. Unless, he's not really dead. What if he really was having one of those near-death experiences? He did after all say he was in some room when he vanished.

Lennox thought for a moment. The sudden anger she had on her face softened. After staring at the ground for a while, she shook her head. "I don't know."

"What'd he look like?"

She narrowed her eyes at him. "Why? Like Zanniel said, does it matter?"

"Damn straight."

Before anyone could say anything else, he explained himself. "'Er's a chance ah ain't dead."

How could he know that? "You were stabbed to death, weren't you?" I pointed out.

"Don't mean ah died. Jus', means ah got injured."

I realized then that the rain had stopped. What was strange, is that we were all as dry as we were before it even began. It didn't even look like it had even rained. Did any of them notice this, too? Probably not. They were more interested in what Clyde was saying. "Ah was in a room. Ah was here an' there at the same time. Don't know how. There were doctors in blue suits an' such an' ah kept hearin' 'em say 'clear.'"

Lennox gasped. "You were in a hospital."

I rolled my eyes at her. "No shit, captain obvious."

"That's insane" said Tristan with sudden excitement. "That means you could possibly catch her killer."

"Thing is," responded Clyde, "ah might *know* 'er killer."

Were they really discussing this? Did Lennox's killer really matter right now? How did we switch topics from Clyde's bad deeds to bringing Lennox's killer to justice? Either way, how could he possibly go about catching him? What proof did Clyde have?

Lennox ran her hands through her blonde hair and realized that it was dry. She inspected her whole body but didn't say anything about it. "Why do you think you know him?"

"Saw 'im with Destiny, didn't ya?"

She shook her head. "I don't follow."

Clyde sighed with frustration. "'Kay. Ah was suppose' to be there with Destiny. The dinner. But after chasin' this Satchel guy, ah knew ah wasn' gonna make it in time. A frien' a' mine was visitin' from Santa Fe. Very same frien' ah tol' Destiny to take with 'er to that dinner seein' as ah wasn' gonna make it in time."

Lennox suddenly looked excited. Not in a happy way, more of a I-can't-believe-this-is-happening sort of way. "What you're saying is that you were supposed to be at my rehearsal dinner with Destiny? I was supposed to meet you that night?"

Clyde nodded in agreement. "Looks it. Don't it?"

"But instead, you were too busy chasing down Satchel because he ran Axel off the road right after he killed Zanniel."

Wow… My jaw dropped. Did I really connect this many lives the night Satchel snapped? How was that possible? I thought back to Lennox's "chain reaction" and was a little unsettled by the fact that we were connected in such ways.

"What-did-he-look-like?" Clyde looked like he was getting frustrated. I'd be, too. No one asked Lennox to play detective.

"He ummm," she struggled a little, "tall, black hair, black eyes, ummm…piercings on his lips, his ears…" Her voice was breaking. She played with her hands and didn't look anywhere but the ground. "Glasses, tan skin…"

Clyde looked past frustrated—he looked angry. "CJ."

"So, his name is CJ," I piped up. "Cool. Go do your police work and arrest him.

"Oh, wait!" My sarcasm was more obvious, "that's right. We're in Limbo. And I'm pretty sure he's not anywhere around here. But you might be alive. Right, officer?"

I knew I wasn't helping the situation. If anything, I was making Clyde even *angrier*. Good. "So, if you live, what? You're going to arrest this CJ character with allegations that he threw Lennox to her death because you happened to encounter her spirit in Limbo while having a near-death experience where she told you all about it. How does that hold up in court?"

I wasn't wrong. What proof did Clyde have that Lennox was killed? This CJ he speaks of could easily say she committed suicide and jumped to her death. He could even say he knew nothing about it and walk away a free man. This lot was idiotic to think they could bring someone to justice. Tristan nodded slowly as I elaborated. "It's impossible. You can't prove anything. You'll sound crazy."

"*Thank you,*" I told Tristan. Clyde's eyes darted back and forth from Tristan and me. He knew I was right. Lennox just stayed looking down and shifted her weight.

So, now what? The connections that all of our fates shared had been brought to light. Axel was gone and so was Satchel. What else needed to happen for one of us to cross over? I remembered Tristan hadn't said what *he* did to put himself in this situation. I turned to him. "You."

"Me?" He was caught off guard. "What about me?"

"What did you do?"

He looked around. Either he was playing stupid, or he didn't know what I meant. "What do you mean?"

I sighed. "What did you do to put yourself in Limbo? There's date rape and baby killer over there, Satchel was a psychopath, and Axel caused his brother's death. And you?"

He twisted his jaw and thought for a moment. "It's acquiescence." He turned to me and I raised an eyebrow. "Come on, Zanniel, face it. We weren't exactly saints. You turned my life around, yes, but anything you had me doing, I did it without question. Even when we outed Fletcher, I did nothing to stop it."

I didn't need him to explain further. I knew exactly what he meant. He never told me "no" nor did he ever contradict me. The most obedient robot of them all. And practically another version of me, except without leadership. I thought back to the day we outed Fletcher. Tristan never said we were doing wrong. He never tried talking me out of it. I gave an order and he did it.

Lennox broke her silence. "You're right."

She was crying now. *Again.* "He's right. There's nothing we can do." That was random. Was that all she was thinking about while Tristan and I shifted topics? Her killer?

I heard Clyde give a loud grunt. We all turned to him and saw he had fallen to his back once more. He was in the same state as before. Squirming, fading in and out, and the electric currents moved through his body again. They were probably trying to save him at the hospital he said he was in.

Lennox moved past me and headed toward Clyde. Wind picked up around us again, but this time something was different. Looking at the factory in front of me, the lights turned off. As I looked closer, the edges of the building began to chip off into small pieces and float up in the air. It looked like it was disintegrating. Apparently, anything can happen in Limbo. And just when I thought I'd seen enough abnormal things, *this* happens.

I looked around and saw that everything else was disintegrating. The trees, Clyde's squad car, even the leaves and pebbles were floating away into nothing. Tristan looked scared to death. Should we run? Get out of here? But where to? Back to downtown? Was there something past downtown left to explore? Too many questions rushed into my head and I didn't feel like I had any time to answer a single one.

The foggy substance became intertwined with the wind so it became harder to see. But I could make out Lennox a few feet in front of me squatted next to Clyde's jolting body. What was she doing? It looked like she was saying something to him. I doubt Clyde could hear anything right now and I had a gut-feeling that Clyde wasn't going to be around much longer.

My body acted before I could think. I lunged toward Lennox and pulled her up. "We have to go!" She didn't resist. She got up with ease and I let her go as she followed me. I started to run and so did Lennox and Tristan. We sprinted up to the hill we came from and found ourselves standing on the road. Once we were away from the sudden distortion, we looked back and saw everything covered in the fog.

We couldn't see the factory anymore. Nothing at all as a matter of fact. Both Lennox and Tristan were wide-eyed staring down. Where we stood, it was still. No noise, no wind, just silence. We looked down quietly. I had nothing to say. Well, I did. But decided to keep quiet. I wasn't sure what exactly happened down there. All I know is Clyde was gone. Heaven, hell, or even back on earth, I didn't know for sure. Either way, that just left the three of us.

XIII

Vexation

Two months after Jason's state basketball party.

The Metropolitan Athletics Recognition Award, better known as MARA is the most wanted and the most difficult award to obtain throughout high school. The MARA is awarded once a year to a male and female senior who have participated all four consecutive years of high school in at least four different varsity programs. In other words, at least sixteen varsity programs throughout their high school career with a minimum of four per year. Said seniors who win the award go in the high school hall of fame. Their jersey numbers get retired, they get a walk on spot to a college athletic program of their choice, scholarship money, and lots of other minor shit. Basically, the winners get fame like they never dreamed of.

Our athletic department was hosting its annual farewell banquet at the school. The dress code was business casual. I wore a black button up, grey blazer, and dark jeans. I picked up Tristan, who wore a khaki blazer over a black button up and matching pants. Clothing that I didn't mind lending from my closet.

We were meeting our other friends at the banquet. I hadn't really spoken to Fletcher since our incident at Jason's. Though it happened almost two months ago, it felt like it happened last night. In fact, I was practically avoiding him all together. As far as I was concerned, nothing happened that night.

The parking lot was already full by the time we pulled in. Everyone who participated in athletics was here tonight. Everyone from the cheerleaders to the golfers. Rio Grande High's athletic programs offered a lot of variety, which made it that much more difficult to be the winner of the MARA.

After we parked and headed toward the gym, I ran into my ex, Jauni. No doubt she was going for that award as well. With varsity cheerleading, track, swimming, and volleyball, she had a fair shot. She looked hot as ever with her brown hair up in a bun. She had blonde highlights in her hair since I first met her, which she would touch up now and then. She had a face like a porcelain doll, and always wore her favorite shade of lipstick: maroon. Tonight she wore black dress, and black heels. She saw me and made her way toward me.

"Hi, Zanniel!" She was always smiling. She reached for a side hug and I lightly hugged her back. "You bring Trinity?"

I chuckled to myself. "Nah. We ended a while ago."

"Oh," she tried to sound surprised, but I felt like she already knew I was single. "I'm sorry to hear that. You should've seen her at state, their cheer team crashed and burned."

"It's whatever," I told her, not acknowledging the cheer part.

We made small talk about her wearing a dress, which she hated doing. She filled me in about drama with some of her fellow cheerleaders, the cheer team getting a different coach for the third time this year, and her getting her nose pierced. I just nodded in agreement at everything she said.

As we entered the gymnasium, Jauni saw her fellow team members and waved me goodbye. "Text me later," she said before taking off. I smiled in agreement, though I wasn't planning on doing it. I already knew what to expect from Jauni, I wasn't looking to get back with her. I looked around for my friends in the group of students.

Tristan elbowed me as he pointed to a table in the middle. Found 'em. We made our way over and sat on the seats assigned. I felt my stomach turn when I saw my name card next to Fletcher's. Of course, that would happen. I took a deep breath and sat down.

I didn't know how Fletcher could act so normal around me. Like nothing happened. In a way I was glad, it saved us from an awkward situation. But, at the same time it was frustrating because I wanted to know what was going on in his head. I refused to ask him about it, however. He could be gay if he wanted. But, I knew I wasn't going to be.

We did a lot of group talking amongst the table and I only spoke directly to Fletcher when necessary and he did the same. Though there was slight tension in the air, the only one who knew about it was Tristan. His eyes would dart back and forth between us. He knew Fletcher had kissed me that night. He came to me about it the day after the party. I denied it at first, but then he pulled out his phone and showed me a picture of us with our lips locked, I almost kicked his ass.

He thought it was funny. But I found no humor. He only knew of the kiss, not what followed. I told him Fletcher was drunk and laid one on me. In the picture, it was obvious that Fletcher was leaned in toward me, so my story had slight proof. Still, I didn't like the idea of Tristan having something on me. Not that he would ever do anything to put me in a predicament, but still.

The small talk around the table continued as it normally would any other day with random topic changes. Red was apparently sleeping with one of Jauni's friends, Whitney. Clemont got accepted to Harvard. He wasn't planning on going—he just wanted to see if he would get accepted or not. Jason was planning a party after the banquet dinner. Nolan talked about getting a promotion at his work… I don't know, something like that; I tuned him out. Tristan was debating what fraternity at UNM he should rush for. Fletcher was deciding whether he should stay in Albuquerque and go to UNM or go down to Cruces with his brother at New Mexico State.

Everything seemed so normal. Why was I so freaked, then? Okay, fine, I had sex with Fletcher. It happened. But why was I so stuck on it? I kept thinking about that party at Jason's. We were drunk, yes, but we both knew exactly what we were doing. I mean, I wasn't gay, I liked chicks. I know I did. I never once found myself checking out any of my other friends. That's just gross. Let alone sleep with them, even more gross.

So then why Fletcher? What came over me that night? He didn't force me to do anything; I was willing, which was the unsettling part. I was brought back from my memories from Clemont's snapping fingers in my face. "Earth to Zanniel?"

"I…" I struggled, "what?"

"I'll take that response as an indication that you didn't attend our last conversation."

I chuckled lightly. "My bad, Clemont. Got other things on my mind."

His eyes widened with excitement behind his glasses. "Things that hold more value than the MARA? Care to incorporate the rest of us in those thoughts?"

No, I thought to myself. Tristan came to my rescue. "That's insane. The MARA's the only thing on Zanniel's mind."

Red scoffed. "Please, that award practically has Zanniel's name on it already."

"Probably," piped up Nolan, "but it's fair game. Anyone can get it if they meet the requirements."

He meant himself. "Yes, Nolan. Let's not forget you got a chance to play varsity basketball freshman year thanks to me, which makes you eligible."

He stared at me with glaring eyes from across the table. "I'm just saying."

"Well don't. Do me a favor and stop bleaching your bangs already. No one ever said it was a good look for you." I smiled at him and he threw me a mocking smile back.

"That may be true," continued Clemont, "but there are several factors that play a supporting role in the MARA. An individual must participate in at least four varsity programs per school year. Zanniel exceeded that every year. Let's see, football, soccer, basketball, wrestling, swimming, cross country and technically track. Not to mention Zanniel's practically the poster child for Rio Grande High. Let's not forget, A average."

Whenever Clemont spoke, I couldn't help but feel like I was getting lectured. "Thank you for reviewing my accomplishments, Clemont. When I die, I'll be sure to have you write my biography."

"Hey," said Jason, "if you're not dating Trinity anymore. She up for grabs?"

That was a change of topic. "Yeah, whatever, man," I said coolly. "Careful though, I can still feel her teeth." I placed my hands over my groin and moved my shoulders inward.

Everyone at the table laughed. Everyone except Fletcher. Was he jealous? One way to find out. I turned to Red. "How was Whitney, fire crotch?"

"Mmmm," he thought, "like, in bed?"

"No," I replied sarcastically, "like in chair."

Red laughed a little. "Not bad, dude. A better job than my hand, that's for sure. What about you? Who you smashing now?"

"No one yet. Was thinking about hitting up Jauni again." I turned to Fletcher. "What do you think?"

My question didn't completely catch him off guard. He already had a sour look on his face. "I dunno," he mumbled, "do who you want."

Before I could go into further detail about girls, the athletic director began giving his speech. Coach Roux looked way too young for his age. The man looked like he was in his early twenties when he was pushing fourty. I guess it's what happens when you stay in shape. Students often said he could pass for my older brother, having the same skin tone and hair color. Coach Roux started off his speech by welcoming everyone and saying what an amazing year it'd been, blah blah blah.

Also, being the boys' basketball varsity coach, he began giving us our awards for a successful season. He went off on a speech about how teamwork helped us take state this year. After more boring speeches were given by other department coaches, it was time for the MARA, the real award.

"As you all know," said Coach Roux, "every year, it is my proud duty to award the Metropolitan Athletic Recognition Award to one lucky male and female athlete. All of you have done an outstanding job of showing

school spirit and representing your Raven Pride at every event. This year was extremely close, as we had several athletes excel not only in dedication, but perseverance as well as hard work."

Everyone in the gym was silent. They were all grasping on to every word he was saying. The anticipation was growing. I was one hundred percent sure that the MARA was going to be mine. It had to be. I tried to control my breathing so that when my name was called, I wouldn't be out of breath.

"Without further ado," he continued, "the MARA award for the female division of this year, goes to your very own Jauni Roybal!"

The crowd went into applause as Jauni got up from her table and made her way up to the podium by coach. He handed her a glass plaque and she posed with it for a photographer from the Albuquerque Journal. Jauni had an overjoyed smile on her face. Her cheeks were so red from blushing that I wondered if she was going to cry. I rolled my eyes at the thought.

"Miss Roybal," he asked, "which athletic program are you walking on to in your college career?"

Jauni leaned over to the microphone and exclaimed, "Co-ed cheerleading!"

The crowd went into an applause yet again. Yes, yes, we get it. Congrats, Jauni. Can we move it along?

"Best of luck, Miss Roybal," continued coach Roux. "Now, the boys." Everyone began stomping their feet at a rapid pace to build on the anticipation even more. I kept my feet still. We weren't kids anymore, why act like it?

"Interesting year it's been as there were several of you that showed not only me, but the other coaches here at Rio Grande just how much you wanted this. But as we all know, there could only be one. This young man has worked hard and has a very promising future ahead of himself. This year, the MARA award in the male division goes to…"

The feet rumbling grew louder. Would he hurry up and say it already?

"… Fletcher Jarvis!" The crowd went into an applause as well as cheers. Standing ovations left and right. My eyes went wide. I turned to Fletcher and he was in shock. Not too much shock because he stood up with no problem. He had a wide-open smile across his face. He rushed to the podium where

he got a plaque handed to him and his photo taken. My friends weren't clapping. Well, Nolan was, but he was irrelevant. They all were looking at me with the same what-just-happened look.

My chest was heaving and my hands balled into fists. "What sick joke is this?" I spat out only loud enough for my table to hear. A lump formed in my throat. I felt like the room was spinning. I no longer heard the crowd of people. Instead, I just heard ringing in my ears. This wasn't happening. I work my ass off all throughout high school and get shit? No. This wasn't fair. Not by a long shot.

"Mister Jarvis," Coach Roux asked Fletcher, "which athletic program are you walking onto in your college career?"

Fletcher couldn't find words. He shrugged his shoulders and smile. "I have no idea! I guess we'll wait and see!"

Like Jauni, Fletcher's cheeks were pink. I felt humiliated. How could Fletcher win an award that was destined to mine? I got up from my seat and turned to Tristan. "Let's go."

I made my way through the crowd not looking back. By the door, there were glasses of what appeared to be apple cider. They probably for the ending toast all the athletes were supposed to drink to. I grabbed one on my way out, chugged it and threw the glass across the hall shattering it. I heard Tristan's footsteps coming up behind me. I heard more people following now that I listened closely.

"That was systematic," said Tristan. "How did Fletcher win?"

"Don't care," I lied.

"Hold up!" Called Jason behind me. I kept walking. "Zanniel!"

I felt someone put their hand on my shoulder and I yanked myself out of their grasp as I turned. It was Red. "Dude!" he exclaimed.

I sighed. "What?"

He pointed back toward the gymnasium. "That was unexpected."

"No shit."

He was enjoying the situation. "You going to Jason's?"

"No. Tristan and I have work to do for the morning paper."

Tristan's eyebrows furrowed but he didn't object. He knew better.

"See you guys in the morning for zero hour," I told them as I turned away and headed toward the exit. Only Tristan followed me then.

Fletcher was going down, I thought to myself, but how? I needed to hit him where it hurt. I needed to put him in a position where he had no escape. A little bit more than just a prank. But what… Once we were back at my place, we changed out of our banquet clothes and threw on shorts and tees.

"So…" tried Tristan, "what's the headline going to be?"

And then I thought of the perfect plot. "Closeted Gay Accepts MARA."

Tristan laughed. "That's hilarious."

I didn't laugh. "It's the truth."

Tristan stopped his giggling. "Wait, you're serious?"

"Of course, I am!" I went to my dresser and retrieved my phone. I needed a little more evidence to go off of other than the picture Tristan had of the kiss. I didn't want to, but I composed a text to Fletcher.

Congrats dude

All I had to do was get Fletcher to confess a few things to me. It didn't take long for him to respond.

Thanks! :) I still can't believe it! Not at Jason's?

Leave it to Fletcher to act like nothing's wrong. I need to get him to confess to me, to open up. But how? Do I go straight for it, or ease my way in? Decisions…

Nah. Not tonight. Fletch, question…

He didn't respond as fast as his first text which made a little nervous. I was digging for dirt I could use against him, yes. But, at the same time, I wanted to know how he really felt about things. We haven't really talked since that night let alone about what happened that night. Tristan was studying me closely. "What are you doing?"

"Just getting proof," I assured him. Before long, Fletcher texted back.

Anything dude. Ask away

I suddenly felt scared, almost guilty. Not for what I was about to discover, but I was going to do with the information. I'd never felt this much hate for Fletcher. How could he take something from me that he knew I really wanted? Friends didn't do that. With that mere thought, the guilt was gone. Why should I feel guilty? If Fletcher really was gay, then he had to own up to it. Not to me, but to the whole school. Here goes.

I feel like you like me more than a friend. Am I wrong?

I sent the text without hesitation. My heart was beating faster than normal and I suddenly started sweating a little. Tristan could tell I was in a funk. He laughed and threw himself on my bed. "It's unclear. What exactly are you planning to do?"

I grabbed a pillow and smacked him across the head with it. "Keep up, freckles! Don't you get it?"

"No, eyebrows, I don't."

He threw the pillow back at me. He hit a nerve talking about my eyebrows, he knew how I felt about them. Dick, I thought to myself. Whatever, I let it slide. "Fletcher just won the MARA, good for him. He'll be front page news on the morning paper. But, I'm going to give a little more details about him than necessary."

"His sexuality?"

"Exactly."

He rubbed his head. "Isn't that like, cyber bullying? Calling him out on his sexuality by forms of media? Won't we get in trouble?"

I checked my phone to see if Fletcher texted back, he hadn't. "Not at all. Trust me, dude. You know how good I am with words. I'll write an article about him winning the MARA, but I'll also include some bullshit about embracing our sexuality. To be proud and what not."

He didn't look convinced, but I got my point across. "And, why? Exactly?"

Oh, Tristan. So gullible. "Why not? Rio Grande will be ready to praise and cheer for their latest MARA winner. I want to make sure they know who exactly it is they're cheering for. You still have that picture you took of us?"

He yawned. "Yeah."

I kicked him on his side and he let out a soft grunt. "Dumbass! I told you to delete it."

Well, it's a good thing he didn't. I needed it now more than ever. I checked my phone, still no reply. "Send it to me."

He pulled out his phone. "Yes, your highness," he said.

My phone vibrated. I looked at it expecting it to be the picture. But, it was Fletcher.

You know, you're right. I don't know what it is Zanniel, you drive me crazy. I don't feel like that toward anyone. Not Jason, Red, Tristan or any of our other friends. I don't know if you feel the same and I know it sounds very gay, but I've really fallen for you. Like for reals. Not sure when, why, or how. But I have. <3

He sent me much more than I could've asked for. I took a screenshot of the texts and grabbed my laptop. I started typing a fast pace. I got everything I needed now. Not only did he tell me his feelings, he opened up the closet door for the whole school to see. Fletcher Jarvis, my dear friend, you're going down.

XIV

Astray

After staring numbly at the cloudy remains of the unknown factory and Clyde, I was over it. I glanced to either side of me at Lennox and Tristan, and they were still staring without a clue. I began walking away from them, knowing they would start following me in a matter of seconds. So, Clyde was gone. Who was next?

After a few steps, Lennox called out. "Hey?!"

I didn't answer. I just kept walking. Where to go? Back to downtown? The storage units? Or should I keep going to see where else I end up? I followed the road that would take me back downtown. Unless I saw something useful, I was going to keep walking. I heard Lennox's heels and Tristan's footsteps close behind. Of course they would follow.

"That was astonishing," said Tristan as he picked up the pace to walk next to me. "Now what?"

Why would he assume that I knew what to do? I didn't. I was clueless, as a matter of fact. But, I didn't show it. I kept looking straight with my face hard. "Guess we'll find out."

Lennox picked up the pace to and pulled up to my left. She didn't say anything, but I know she wanted to. She must have *something* to say about what we just saw. But I didn't push it. Not yet, anyway.

After a few feet of walking, we passed the train tracks and were back in downtown. I got a glance of the movie theater and a few hotels in the distance. We were back on Central Avenue. But this time, I was not taking detours. I kept walking straight. The foggy substance in the air was still as thick and eerie as it was when I first came by here. I wonder if anyone else was here? I thought about where I encountered Lennox and Axel. Could anyone else be waiting to be found?

As I passed 3rd Street, I saw 4th Street in front of me, but the buildings didn't look like they continued onward. Where was the rest of downtown? As I came up to the cross street, I stopped. The others were close by and stopped at the same point as me.

"Stuck?" Teased Lennox. *Bitch*, I thought to myself. To prove her wrong, I kept walking. I didn't know what was beyond, but oh well. There's bound to be something else out here. Funny enough, the other two followed me. Talk about rudderless.

We walked in silence. No one said anything, nor did they make sounds other than their footsteps. There was nothing around us but fog. The only thing visible was the road and I could barely see a few feet in front of me. Was there nothing beyond 4th Street? Should I turn around? I wanted to go back, but my body kept going. I had a suspicion that there was something out here.

After a few more feet, I saw a sign up ahead. I couldn't make out what it said just yet, but the excitement of encountering something new had me walking faster. As soon as I picked my pace, I began slowing down as the sign became clear. The black sign with red letters read *Rio Grande High School.* Right underneath it said *Home of the Ravens.*

I was dumbfounded. Why was I at my old high school? I looked around to see if there was anything else, anything I might've missed. There wasn't. I turned to Tristan as he came up next to me, and he had the same facial expression. "That's not weird at all."

"No shit," I replied. Lennox crossed her arms as she came up next to us. This time she didn't stay quiet.

"Okay, any idea why we're here of all places?"

I sighed in frustration. "Yeah, Lennox. There's a bulletin board up ahead with a very detailed explanation."

My sarcasm didn't bother her. "There might be." She walked ahead of us and onto the campus. She looked around but kept a steady pace as she headed toward the entrance. I knew this school like the back of my hand. The halls, the classrooms, everything. Part of me wanted to go explore. Another part of me wanted to wait to see if the doors were locked like those downtown. As Lennox approached the entrance, she pulled on the doors and they opened without problem. She turned back to us as if to say, you guys coming?

I glanced at Tristan and then headed toward the entrance. He followed close by. Once we got in through the double doors, the rush of familiarity came through me. Four years I attended this school. In those years, I gained the respect of others, followed by envy, admiration, and everything else. Everyone knew me. Thanks to me, everyone knew Tristan as well as those other leaches known as my friends. I ruled this place and everyone that attended.

The halls were empty. The black and red lockers were all shut. Everything was in order except for a bunch of papers scattered all over the floor. As I looked more closely, they were scattered *everywhere*. As I picked one up, I recognized it immediately. I felt a cold shiver run down my spine as I looked at the article I wrote about Fletcher. Tristan picked one up, too, as did Lennox.

Was this why we were here? Because of Fletcher and his suicide? Lennox looked like she was deeply interested as she read through the article. How long before she came at me with another lecture?

After a few moments of reading, Lennox turned to me. "Why would you do this?"

"It was jealousy," said Tristan. I turned and scowled at him. "What? It's true."

"Because he got the MARA instead of you? Was that it?" She said it in an I-can't-believe-you tone. She wouldn't understand. She didn't know anything about my life to even begin to comprehend how badly

I wanted that award. She didn't know how hard I worked, the time and effort, nothing. She knew *nothing*.

I didn't answer her. I stared back at her appalled look. "He trusted you, he basically worshipped you. And you stabbed him in the back."

I shifted uncomfortably. Her words were getting to me. My chest was heaving and, if I wasn't mistaken, it felt like I was going to cry.

"I don't think people should take justice into their own hands," she continued, "but, I can understand now why Satchel wanted you dead."

I'd had enough. My body acted before my mind could react. I found myself running. Not necessarily running away from Lennox and her words, but rather running toward something. Not just something, someplace: the pool facility. The last place I saw Fletcher. I sprinted so fast that the newspaper articles seemed to fly up by my sides. I didn't look back nor did I stop for any reason.

I exited the halls and ran into the patio area in front of the gym. It was still hard to see, but I knew where I was going. I kept running until I was at the pool entrance. I paused for a second at the entrance then ran inside. I looked around briefly for anything out of place. Once everything looked to be normal, I went to the pool. As I looked around the floor, I saw the familiar sight of the shattered glass, the torn letterman jacket, and the shredded certificates. Once I passed the doors into the pool, there it was. I fell to my knees and found myself bawling. I gave small sobs at first, then they instantly grew louder. I balled my fist and punched the tiled floor.

"Fletcher!" I screamed at the top of my lungs. I looked up to the ceiling and saw the water ripples being reflected. Right in the center, just past the diving board, was the rope. The same rope I saw Fletcher hanging from that morning and the exact rope that, thanks to my actions, took my best friend's life.

XV

Eradicated

The day after the MARA distribution.

"Bright futures," read Clemont, "and promising opportunities come forth to this year's annual Metropolitan Athletic Recognition Award winners. Seniors Jauni Roybal and Fletcher Jarvis were announced as MARA representatives for Rio Grande High.

"Let us not forget, Ravens. Just as these seniors proudly accept their award with great pride, one must also accept themselves with just as much, if not more, pride. One thing that is commonly overlooked by the means of popularity labels is a person's sexuality. Rio Grande has an excellent LGBTQ program but it isn't accessed by those who need it most. MARA winner Fletcher Jarvis has had a constant struggle but has finally accepted himself for who he truly is.

"Senior Zanniel Zephyr saw firsthand just how wrong people were to assume that Jarvis was of the straight orientation. Zephyr has no future plans of undergoing a romantic relationship with Jarvis even though both heart and soul were put out to be seen.

"Zephyr was completely caught off guard as Jarvis not only physically imposed his desires (as seen on the photographs) but also admitted his feelings via text message when asked about it.

"Had Jarvis reached out for help by LGBTQ members, he might have had a smoother transition into exposing his feelings. Zephyr says he's not mad nor does he have anything against his best friend. Jarvis is encouraged *to continue his lifestyle as he chooses with the only condition being he does it the right way.*

"As the student body, let us encourage everyone to be themselves and welcome them out of the closet. Those who feel the need to stay inside said closet should see that it is a brighter place outside. We are one school, one community, and one of a kind, Ravens. Let us not forget that together we fly and no Raven will be left behind."

"Is that real?" Asked Red as he turned the computer his way. "You kissed Fletcher?"

"Correction, Red," I clarified, "he kissed me."

"Gay," said Jason. "I like how you interviewed yourself."

"Wait," said Clemont, "you're seriously publishing this? The student body's going to eat Fletcher alive. You know how close-minded they can be."

"Exactly," I noted. We were gathered in the journalism office. Clemont, Red, Jason, Tristan, Nolan, and myself. I texted Fletcher earlier and told him not to come to zero hour. I didn't respond to his last text the night before. He ended up sending the same text again about an hour later but gave up waiting for my response. Even this morning, all he responded was "K."

"Back up," said Jason. "Why exactly are you so suddenly eager to ruin Fletcher?"

The computer monitor went black. After I looked to the side, I saw Nolan's hand on the power switch. He was looking at me with a serious face. I dismissed Jason's question and focused on Nolan. "Nolan, get your paw off the monitor."

He didn't answer right away. He seemed to be choosing his words. "I don't think you should do this."

Was he telling me what to do? Not directly, but physically he was trying to stop me. "I didn't ask for your input. Now back off."

I tried to move his hand out of the way, but he kept a firm grip. Was he seriously trying to defy me? Me? The one who made his whole high school career better by befriending him? He was starting to piss me off. I was taking deep breaths to keep from hitting him. He just stared at me with the same look.

"To answer your question, Jason," he finally spoke, "Zanniel is clearly upset about last night, seeing as Fletcher won the MARA instead of him. So, Zanniel's trying to get back at Fletcher by humiliating him in front of the entire school, because he doesn't like losing."

Without thinking twice, I spat in his face. Out of instant reaction, Nolan took a swing and smacked me across the face. With more force, I returned the punch at his face, making him cry out in pain. Bet he wishes he would've let go of the switch when I told him to.

I felt someone hold my arm back. It was Tristan. Clemont got up and went to check on Nolan. Red got in the middle. "Hey, hey, hey," he said nervously. "Come on man, it's too early for that."

I ignored him. I kept egging Nolan on. "Say something else."

I heard him whimper. Clemont looked up at me. "I think you broke his nose."

Good, I thought. Serves him right. "Take him to the nurse," I instructed Clemont. "Meet us at the locker hall in an hour."

Nolan got up holding his nose. Blood was all over his lower chin. He gave me a quick glare and then left the room followed by Clemont. I turned the monitor back on and continued with the printing process. Jason leaned over the desk. "Hey, won't we get in trouble for this?"

"Yeah, Zanniel," agreed Red, "this is funny and shit, but—"

"Then what are you waiting for?" I interrupted. "If it's so funny, laugh."

Red just stared. Tristan felt the tension and spoke up. "It's brilliant."

We all turned to him. "Don't you guys see? Zanniel is putting Fletcher on blast but the way he worded his whole article puts him in a respected position. He can't get any trouble from it because he's telling everyone to love themselves. To open up with pride and all that other crap. He's not technically singling Fletcher out. He's using him as the example, and he has the pictures to prove it."

Always to my rescue, Tristan was. I never thanked him for having my back. My friendship to him was enough of a thanks as far as I was concerned. But he knew exactly how I was approaching this entire article. I get the concerns my friends were having. But, I had all our backs covered.

They didn't ask any more questions nor did they object. We began getting the papers ready and within no time, my friends headed off to drop off the papers around campus. I checked the clock and it was 7:10. My friends left the office at 6:30; the entire school should have that paper in their hands by now. I grabbed my backpack and headed for the lockers. First period starts in twenty minutes. Fletcher should be getting here any moment.

As I entered the halls, students were already reading the paper. My plan was going exactly as planned. Heads turned as I passed. They always did. I knew I was putting myself in the red by being exposed as the guy that Fletcher was kissing. But I held my head high. It was Fletcher that was going to get attacked, not me.

I got to the lockers and saw my friends huddled together. As I got closer, I saw a few bandages on Nolan's nose. Everyone was in a better mood than this morning. Even with a busted nose, Nolan threw me a soft smile as I joined them as a welcome. No sign of Fletcher. I checked my phone to see if he'd texted me. He hadn't.

"Damn," said Jason with excitement, "Fletcher has no idea what he's walking into."

"What happens after the fact?" asked Clemont. "After Fletcher gets here and sees everything?"

I sighed. "We have a big laugh then move on with our lives." Fletcher's locker and all our friends' were in the same section. Fletcher was bound to pass by here. I checked the time. 7:17. Where was he?

As if on cue, I heard running footsteps come up behind me. I turned and saw Fletcher with a shocked look on his pale face. He was out of breath and sweating. I felt a smile slowly form on my face. He didn't say anything. He looked around at the others then back at me. Was he about to cry?

"Hey, Skittles," joked Red and we all burst out in laughter.

Fletcher wasn't having it. He looked like was going to pass out. The misery on his face wasn't enough; I pushed it further. I stepped closer to him. "Kiss and make up?"

My friends laughed even harder. This time Fletcher retaliated. He gave me a shove to my chest that I hit the lockers behind me. He was mad all right. To make things worse, I taunted him further by puckering my lips and blowing him a kiss. He came at me with a grunt of frustration. He grabbed me by jacket and threw me down. I pulled him down, too. This turned into a fight. Fletcher was throwing blows at my face. They didn't hurt; they felt like girl punches.

I grabbed him by his waist and flipped him over. I was returning the punches back now. A few seconds into the spontaneous brawl, I got lifted up. I turned and saw Coach Roux with an angry look on his face. "Hey!" he yelled. "That's enough!"

Nolan went to help Fletcher up but he pulled away and got up on his own. Students had gathered around to see what the commotion was all about.

"Jarvis," instructed Coach Roux, "my office. Now." He pointed to the end of the hall where his office was. But, Fletcher grabbed his bag and turned the other way. Once the other students made way for him to pass, he took off running without saying a word.

"Run, fag!" called out Jason. Take that, Fletcher.

Talk about an eventful day. After mine and Fletcher's little incident, my parents got a call from coach. What was this? Elementary school? Anyways, my parents tried lecturing me as we sat and ate dinner. I dismissed their concerns and the lecture all together by saying we were just messing around. And they left it at that.

Fletcher was the talk of the whole school. People couldn't believe he'd been in the closet all this time. I did feel a slight sense of guilt for only publishing part of the story. But they didn't need to know the rest.

The doorbell rang and I instantly got up to answer. Dinner with my parents was awkward. It rarely happened, and when it did, it was uncomfortably quiet. I couldn't have gotten up and away faster. When I opened the door, I saw Fletcher standing outside. It was raining aggressively and he wasn't wearing a jacket. He was soaked.

He didn't say anything. He just stared at me miserably with his arms crossed over his chest. Did he want an apology? An invitation inside? A jacket?

"Hey," I tried. He didn't respond. I shifted my weight and tried again. "Wanna come in, dude?"

Still nothing. Okay…so why was he here then? I heard someone coming up behind me. "Fletcher!" exclaimed my mom. "What are you doing? You're going to catch pneumonia. Come inside. I made dinner."

If Fletcher wasn't talking before, he definitely wasn't about to start now. I wanted to shove her and tell her to go away, but Fletcher spoke. "No, thanks, Miss Z. I have to get going."

"Oh," she sighed, "well, hurry home! You shouldn't be out in this weather." After that, she turned away and went back to the kitchen. Fletcher just stared at me again. His black bangs covered his eyes and I wasn't sure if he was crying or not; he was too wet from the rain.

"I'm sorry," he finally said. Sorry? I just outed him to the entire school and he's the one that's sorry? "I shouldn't be here. I'll go away now." And just like that, he turned and took off running. Where was his car? Why was he on foot? I didn't get a chance to ask. I was going to call after him, but decided against it. He'll talk when he's ready. He'll probably end up thanking me for this in the future.

I went to bed early, too much excitement for one day. About an hour into my sleep, my phone went off, announcing a new text message. I grunted and rolled over to retrieve it from the table on the side of my bed. It was Fletcher.

Hey. Sorry about today. I was out of line. It was wrong for me to have accepted the MARA, too. I called coach and told him it belongs to you. Meet me at the pool tomorrow morning before zero hour? I'll be doing laps and want you to have the plaque ASAP. See you then :)

Talk about random. If he felt that way, why not bring the award when he came to my house? Bipolar much? Whatever. All I responded with was "K." I shut off my phone and went back to sleep.

I woke up around 4 the next morning. I took a quick shower and got ready. After I did my hair, I pulled on my letterman jacket and was on my way to school. Why did he want to meet so early? We had an open-twenty-four-hours pool facility. But, no one ever went that early. I got to school at 5:25—zero hour wasn't until 6. I got there a little early with the intentions of talking things out. I wasn't sure what I really felt for Fletcher. Regardless, he was still my best friend and I didn't like fighting with him.

His car was the only one in the parking lot. No surprise there. I pulled up next to his, then went inside. What do I say? Sorry? I was the never good with apologies. I figured if I ignored a situation long enough, it got better on its own.

The inside was quiet. I didn't hear water splashing. Was Fletcher not swimming? As I looked ahead, I saw there were papers scattered all around. I tilted my head to get a better view. It was yesterday's article. I sighed then proceeded to the pool area. I kept walking and heard a crunching noise. What did I step on? I inspected my shoe and saw that it was glass. Then I noticed there was glass all over the floor. This place was trashed. What happened?

There were glass chunks here and there. As I looked on the floor, there were torn letter patches; the ones you get awarded and put on your letterman jacket. There were pieces everywhere just like the glass. As I got closer to the door, I saw a metal plate and froze when I recognized it. It was the MARA plaque that was given to Fletcher. Did he destroy it?

I put two and two together with the torn patches: they were from Fletcher's jacket. Ugh, Fletcher, what did you do? I passed the double doors to the pool but didn't see Fletcher. All I saw was his torn-up letterman jacket on the floor. I went to look at the last name on the back for confirmation that it was his. "Jarvis." Yup. This was his.

Where the hell was he? I looked around but no one else was here. Then I looked at the glowing pool and noticed the stillness of the water, but there were water drops falling in the center. I slowly looked up to see where they were coming from and I froze in fear.

There was a rope tied to one of the ceiling poles. And hanging from it was Fletcher. I thought I was imagining it. I blinked several times to rid my eyes of the image. But, it didn't go away. His black lifeless eyes were staring blankly from the hanging body. Fletcher. My best friend was dead.

XVI

Revelations

I was finally feeling it: the pain of losing Fletcher. When I was alive, I cared that he hung himself, but I didn't take on any blame. I didn't make him do it, so my conscience was clean. My days carried on like normal. I didn't mourn nor did I go into a state of slight depression like my friends did. Fletcher was gone, that didn't mean the earth stopped spinning. I was good at both hiding my emotions and turning them off completely.

But, acknowledging the rope above me where I last saw Fletcher's lifeless body, I couldn't help but feel responsible. But, I felt more. What was it? Fault? Liable? Guilt? Ugh! Why was I feeling so horrible? My eyes were closed. But as I opened them, I realized I was crying. As I looked at my fist over the tiled floor, I was shaking. What was happening to me?

Something caught my eye in the pool. I thought I was imagining it at first, but there was something there. No, *someone*. They were swimming underneath the surface. As they began to swim in my direction, I had a feeling it was Fletcher. But, how? Then again, this was Limbo. How was anything possible? As they broke through the surface, I saw his black hair fall over his eyes the way it did when he swam. His light skin tone and black eyes. He was even wearing the same red swim trunks he'd had on when I last saw him. Fletcher was in front on me, swimming and looking very much alive. But, I knew he wasn't.

There was a lump in my throat again. Fletcher just stared back at me. Not with a blank expression, but more like he knew a secret. He had his eyebrows raised and the slightest of smiles. Was he waiting for me to say something? To do something? He tilted his head to the side as an indication to get in. He wants me to swim with him? Why?

I stood up and pulled my hooded sweater vest off. I took off my shoes and socks, followed by my pants, leaving only boxer briefs. With a small leap, I dove in. I didn't feel the water on my skin as I got in. I didn't even have to hold my breath. I looked around for Fletcher but didn't see him. I rose to the surface and pulled my bangs out of my eyes to see. But, he wasn't there. I searched around but there was no one in the pool except myself.

Then, a hand came up and covered my eyes. I turned and saw Fletcher. He looked surprised to see me. He looked happy, though. Was he really here? Was I imagining this? He didn't say anything. He went into a backstroke and kicked water my way. Was he playing with me? I swam to him not sure what was going on. But, Fletcher was definitely here.

He turned and dove under. I did the same. Underwater, he was swimming circles around me. He *was* playing with me. He had a smile on his face the whole time. He looked so careless, so *alive*. Then again, he always did. It was strange not having to think about holding my breath; I just swam. After a few cycles of circling around each other, he stopped. I stopped, too. Now what? He kicked his feet and swam upwards. I did the same, but was there a point to this? I was glad to see Fletcher again, but what did this have to do with anything?

Once on top, he embraced me. I hugged him back. I missed Fletcher—I knew I did. I never said it. Never showed it, or expressed my feelings from losing my best friend. He rested his head on my shoulder. I never would've done any of this in public when I was alive. Now, I'll never be able to. But, had I never published that article, what would've become of us? I knew what Fletcher felt toward me, but what about me toward him? I knew there was something there that I never came to terms with. But would we have ended up trying things out? Would we have dated? I already had sex with the guy, what would've stopped me from labeling him as my boyfriend if the opportunity presented itself?

Fletcher lifted his head and looked in my eyes. I felt nervous suddenly. "Can't you talk?" I asked abruptly. He smiled and nodded. Okay…then, why wasn't he? He reached in for a kiss and I let him have it. I ended up kissing him back. He pulled away after a few seconds and put his mouth toward my ear.

"I love you," he whispered. Just then, I heard a voice calling out. It was Tristan. I opened my eyes and realized I was still on my knees on the side of the pool. Did I never dive in? Was Fletcher never here? Did I imagine the whole thing? I looked up at him as he squatted next to me. I looked over at the pool and the water was still. No Fletcher in sight.

"You okay?" he asked. He looked concerned. How long had I been here for? Where was Lennox? He looked up at the rope hanging from the ceiling. "That's unsettling."

I stood up to compose myself. "Right? Where's the parrot?"

He chuckled. "She's in our old homeroom. There's something she wants you to see."

I rolled my eyes and we headed toward the exit. I took one last look at the pool before heading out. I knew I hadn't imagined it. Fletcher was here. He told me he loved me. It got me thinking. Deep down in some strange abnormal way, did I love him back? I'll probably never know. Heaven, hell, I doubt my love life would matter wherever I ended up.

As was got out of the building and headed toward the classrooms, I heard a cracking noise. I turned and saw the pool facility we were just in disintegrating, just like the factory from earlier was. Pieces were chipping off from the top and floating upward. But, it wasn't the same as the factory. There no storm, rain, or chaos of any kind. This time, it was calm. And it was only that part of the school that was leaving, everything else was still intact. Tristan didn't seem to notice it, so I didn't bother telling him.

Tristan lead the way, but I knew where our old homeroom was. Inside, Lennox stood in front of the black chalkboard with her hands on her hips. She had taken her jacket off. She was just in her red halter dress. She reminded me of one of those hot teachers that the guys would drool over. On the board, she had drawn out something that looked like a timeline that had branches breaking off in several directions.

"I've figured it out," she said as she turned to face us. I took a seat in my old desk in the middle row. I put my hands behind my head as I waited for her to explain.

"Let's start here." She drew an X on the part of the line that was titled *Savage Seven* with my name below, followed by all my other friends'. "You were really something here, weren't you? The popular jock that everyone knew. You had the whole school practically eating out of the palm of your hand. You befriended a few guys whose lives you changed drastically. Your 'robots' as others put it. You got them to do anything and everything you wanted. Out of fear, respect, or admiration, it's not clear. But they undoubtedly had your back.

"Moving on." She drew a new X on the line that read *Senior Basketball Game/Party*. "This night is what set off a series of chain reactions, or domino effect, same thing. Just like I had mentioned earlier. I was at that game and party with my friends." She had drawn three branches from that X. Two went up and one went down. On the top branches, she had written *Destiny & Clyde* and the other *Trinity Heartbroken*. The bottom branch had *Fletcher kissed Zanniel.* "It was at this very party that Destiny had met Clyde. He got her pregnant shortly after, and this also set off a chain reaction. But firstly, had you never been dating Trinity in the first place, we never would've been at that party and Clyde would've never came in the picture. Anyways, you broke up with Trinity, putting her in a state of depression that would eventually cause my accident. This is *also* the night that Fletcher showed you how he felt. Where the picture got taken and you were entrusted with his secret.

"A few weeks later"—she drew a new X on a part of the line that read *State Cheer Comp*——"the New Mexico State cheerleading competition takes place. Because of Trinity's broken heart and Destiny's soon to be miscarriage, I fall from a stunt, forcing me to permanently sit out from cheer for the rest of my life.

"A little after," she drew an X on the main line that said *MARA*, "Fletcher gets the award that you deeply desired, causing your jealousy to get the best of you, and you decide to expose his secret to the entire school. Following that"—she drew an X on the line that said *Fletcher's Death*—"he kills himself. That's where Satchel comes in."

She had a branch facing down from the main line reading *Satchel*, and there was a line underneath that one with several points. The first point said *Hospital*, the next said *Plan*, and the last said *Escape*. She marked an X on *Hospital*. "After Fletcher killed himself, Satchel lost it. He quickly drove to Albuquerque from Las Cruces when he heard that his brother had committed suicide. At his mom's, he goes mad and the authorities restrain him and take him in for psychiatric evaluation. Evaluation, at a hospital where a few of your friends worked." On the bottom line before *Plan*, it had Clemont, Jason and Red's names written. "They recognize Satchel and begin to talk with him about Fletcher. Stuck on revenge, Satchel convinces them to help him eliminate the one who caused his brothers' death. They try to recruit the rest of your friends, but Tristan wasn't convinced to take part in it.

"They get Satchel out"—she marked an X on *Escape*—"and he then comes for you with the help of your friends. That same night, I have my rehearsal dinner. A dinner that so conveniently was scheduled the same night you were supposed to leave for Kentucky. Jason made sudden plans for us without me knowing of his hidden agenda. Knowing you would stay that night to say goodbye. That's when Satchel got you."

The bottom point that read *Escape*, connected back with the main one on a point that said *Zanniel & Tristan Dead*. She backtracked to the part that had her cheerleading incident. "Going into *my* life a little, after my incident, I start doing some devious things." She started drawing a new line above the main one. She marked an X entitled *Cat* and another one *Cat Stopped*. "I do my little robberies for a short time until everything catches up to me. This CJ person—that's what Clyde said his name was—was hot on my trail. After he finds me and almost catches me, I escape and end up meeting with Jason, where we begin dating. After my life seems to get back in order, Jason proposes and I end up at my dinner." She connected the top line back to the middle one.

"Now, here's where things get very tangled"—she drew an X on the next point on the line that said *Axel*—"Satchel was driving like crazy and he ended up running Axel off the road, causing his death. Clyde happens to be there to see it happen and goes after Satchel. While Clyde is off doing that, he was unable to attend the dinner with Destiny so CJ ends up going in his place. Once at the dinner, CJ recognizes me immediately and throws me overboard." She marked an X on the next point that said *Lennox's Death*. "While that's happening at my rehearsal dinner, Clyde and Satchel are off killing one another. I'm only assuming that Clyde lived, but we have no way of knowing for sure."

She sets the chalk down and turns toward me. "All this madness that took place was because of *you*, Zanniel. You set everything off. You caused Tristan's death, made Fletcher take his life, caused me to land in a dark place doing dark things that eventually got me killed. After mapping all of this out, I concluded that Axel was just in the wrong place at the wrong time. Same goes for his brother. Satchel never would've gone insane had you never outed his brother to the school. A lot of grief and demise could've been prevented if only you considered what harm your actions would end up doing."

"You *bitch*," I told her as I got up from my seat. She kept the same hard look on her face as I approached her. It was time to let her have it.

"Listen to yourself! Do you know how childish and idiotic you sound? Have you never heard of taking responsibility for your actions? Did I hand Fletcher a rope and tell him to hang himself? No. Did I tell you to go rob guys while you drugged them? No. Did I make Clyde smash your friend Destiny, getting her pregnant? No. Did I make Tristan not take part of the plan to kill me? No. Nor did I force anyone to do any of the things on your stupid list! Things happen, Lennox! You can't control what happens to you, but you *can* control how you react to them!"

I wasn't sure at what point I started shouting. She stared at me like she wanted to say something. I was expecting her to. I knew I wasn't wrong. I was wondering how she knew about the hospital and Satchel's backstory at first. Tristan had mentioned the hospital back when we were at the factory, but I forgot to ask him about it. He obviously knew more about Satchel than he let off. He probably helped Lennox draw out this stupid timeline by filling in the blanks. "If you wanna stand there and blame me for everything you did, then I think you're missing the whole point of Limbo. If you're going to continue to justify your actions, then you deserve to burn in hell."

As I spoke to her, I knew I was right about Limbo because I felt it already. Back at the pool, I learned it. Everything I suppressed, ignored, and dismissed. I knew what I was. Not when I was alive, but I knew it now. I took a deep breath and walked over to the chalkboard. I grabbed an eraser and removed the point that read *Fletcher Kissed Zanniel.* "You're missing a few details."

"And I suppose *you* know all about Limbo now?" She asked, but I ignored her. I wrote on the chalkboard with such anger. How could she blame me for things she did of her own free will? Talk about pathetic. When I was done writing. I turned to Tristan. I didn't let him see what I wrote. I wanted to explain myself first.

"There was more to that night than just the kiss. I couldn't face what happened back then, but I see things differently now. After you passed out, Tristan, Fletcher and I crashed in Jason's parents' bedroom. Only, before we did…we did things."

Tristan's mouth opened slightly and Lennox was looking at me with wide eyes. My voice began breaking a little. "We hooked up that night. By that I mean I had sex with my best friend. I didn't know what it meant and I didn't want to face it after it happened. I was scared. Scared to face my demons if I was gay and scared about what would happen to the life I worked so hard to build. I knew Fletcher felt something for me because I felt it back toward him. I never told anyone what happened that night and neither did Fletcher. We were both confused and still finding ourselves and I left him to explore that world alone."

I moved out of the way and revealed what I wrote. *Zanniel Hooked Up with Fletcher.* That took guts and a shit load of courage. I had their full attention now. Lennox sat back on a desk and crossed her arms. "Any other questions?" I demanded.

"That's crazy," noted Tristan, "it's understandable why you kept it a secret. But, I mean, like, are you gay, or?"

"I don't know *what* I am, dude. I know I lived my life putting labels on everything and everyone. But, I never paid attention to these so called 'feelings' I apparently had toward Fletcher." Things got awkwardly quiet. I was waiting for Lennox to start questioning me. But, she just stared at me. Nothing to say? That's a first.

"So…" said Tristan not meeting my eyes, "were you… the pitcher or the catcher?"

Really? That's what he was wondering? I picked up a chalk and threw it in his direction. "Shut up."

He laughed then. I glanced at Lennox and she had a grin on her face. If all the pieces were now put together, why were we all still here? What's left for us to figure out? I turned my attention to Lennox. "What now?"

She didn't look at me. "I don't know." *That* was helpful. She went to retrieve her denim jacket and put it on. Without saying a word or looking back, she left the room. Where was *she* off to? Tristan and I looked at each other and then went after her. Chasing someone wasn't usually my thing to do. But I didn't see any other reason to hang around at my old high school.

Her heels made loud clinking noises in the empty hall. Was she going to tell us where she was going? Lennox was very good at talking, yet she hadn't said a thing since I threw her lecture back at her. Was she upset? Did she want us to ask? Girls were good at being quiet and expecting guys to ask what was wrong.

Once we got outside the school, Tristan finally said something. "Where are you going?"

Lennox stopped in front of the school and turned to face us. "Where did you go?" She was asking me, not Tristan. "When you took off, where were you?"

Why the sudden interest? "Does it matter?" I hadn't told them anything about seeing Fletcher. I didn't owe either of them an explanation. But she was getting at something. She wasn't asking out of curiosity—her tone told me otherwise. She asked as if she already had part of the answer.

"Actually, it does. Wherever you went or whatever you saw, changed you. Your persona, character, views. Had we been back with Axel and the others, you never would've opened up about sleeping with Fletcher."

She was right. I knew I had felt something back at the pool. Some vigorous connection with my emotions that I'd never felt before. According to Lennox, it had been obvious in my actions. But all I did was encounter Fletcher. The pool wasn't even there anymore. "I think we're supposed to conclude something before we can cross over."

She had a confused look on her face. "Conclude how?"

I sighed, I *guess* I'll explain. "I saw Fletcher. I had this sudden urge to go to where I found his body: the pool. He was there, swimming."

"That's inconceivable," said Tristan, "I didn't see him when I went to get you. What did he say? What did he do?"

"He didn't really say much. We just swam together." I probably sounded insane. When Tristan went to get me, I was dry. I hadn't even gone into the pool from what he saw. But, before they began questioning that, I had to explain. "My point is, I felt something. It sounds really cheesy and I feel really stupid for saying this out loud, but something inside me came to face all the wrong I did to Fletcher. For the first time, I actually started to feel regret toward something I did."

"Okay, then," she said as she turned and started walking away. What was her deal? Tristan started to go after her. I did, too, but a cracking sound behind me had me turning around instead. Rio Grande High School, right before me, was disintegrating into pieces just like everything else before. Small pieces chipped off into the sky before being completely engulfed in the fog.

If my guess about us needing to conclude something was right, that's why these buildings kept vanishing. There was nothing more there that we needed. The car for Axel, and the factory for Satchel and Clyde. I found Fletcher here and he got me to realize the pain I caused; there went the pool. Lennox connected all of us in her poorly drawn timeline; there went the school.

After a few beats, all I was left staring at was the fog. Or haze, or mist. I still didn't know what surrounded us. Clouds maybe? I don't know. Whatever. Point is, there was nothing left to see here. I turned and saw the other two looking this way as well. Lennox's eyes met mine and she immediately turned back and started walking.

"Let's go," I told Tristan as I passed him. How could Lennox walk away like she could possibly know where she was going? She couldn't even see a few feet in front of her. We walked in silence for a few steps when I decided to small talk with Tristan. "Hey, you remember homecoming?"

"That's a flashback." He smiled. "I do. Why?"

"Who'd you vote for?"

"For court?"

Duh, I wanted to say. But refrained from it. "Yes, for court."

"That's random. I voted Jauni for queen and you for king. Why?"

All my friends had said they voted for me. Even Fletcher and Jason who were running as well. Jason got crowned duke, Fletcher prince, and I got king. Though they all said they voted for me; had they really? It was anonymous voting so I have no way of knowing for sure. But these guys *killed* me. Did they really want me as their king? Was our friendship even genuine, or was it all a lie? They hated me. But then again, I deserved to be hated.

"Still there?" he asked me. I was so lost in the memory that I forgot to speak.

"Yeah." I chuckled. "Just thinking. I did a lot of messed up things. I didn't deserve to be king." I wasn't sure where I was going with this anymore. I don't think Tristan did either. We walked silently close behind Lennox. I still wasn't sure what her plan was.

I saw something faintly beyond the fog. I thought it was one of the buildings from downtown, but it wasn't. It was smaller, squared, and the black brick with floor to ceiling windows looked too familiar. Holy shit. This was *my* house.

XVII

WONDERS

I WAS OVERJOYED WITH THE recognition of my house. I ran past Lennox and went straight for my driveway to get a closer view. No cars were parked out front, nor was there any sign of neighboring houses. But, this *was* my house. My friends always said it looked more like a chateau. The two-story black brick house I grew up in. It had vines growing up the sides and a willow tree on our front lawn. I was home.

Or was I? We were still in Limbo and that could mean a lot things. Was my house here for me? Or was it here for Tristan? He did die in my house, after all. Going off my concluding theory, was this where he needed to be for him to cross over?

I wasted no time. I went for the front door and, to my surprise, it was unlocked. I let myself in and started to look around. Everything was the same at it was *before* we got attacked. The lamp I had smashed was still intact on the side of the couch. There was no blood on the floor from either me or Tristan. I went to turn the light on but nothing happened. I could see just fine, I just wanted to see if it worked.

I didn't wait for the others to catch up. I headed upstairs to my bedroom. I went to my dresser to see if the picture of me and my friends was still there. It was. I wanted to destroy it. I went to pick it up and held it up to my face. I got the sense of déjà vu. This is right where I was standing before Tristan and I were attacked. I looked at the faces of my friends. Such happy smiles. They were all *lies*. They hated me.

I lay in my bed and stared at the picture some more. Why did they hate me so much? Aside from Fletcher's suicide, I not only gave them the perfect lives they lived, we did everything together. Let's see, I had us all get matching piercings on our left ears. The industrial was the hype of our generation, and even though my friends were skeptical about it, they all agreed to it.

After we received suspension from one football game as disciplinary action for tagging another school. I got the idea it would be fun to spike up our team's juice jug with alcohol from Jason's cabinet. Once all the players on the field were intoxicated, we were called to forfeit the game. The varsity coach at the time was taken into questioning. He knew that my friends and I were responsible for the incident. But, he had no way of proving how minors got ahold of such alcohol in the first place. He was on paid leave at first, but then resigned his position.

There was this one math teacher our junior year for pre-calculus: Mrs. Anaya. Quite the MILF she was, but a real bitch when it came to grades. Of course, Clemont had the highest grade in the class, but me and my friends were falling behind. Jason had the worst: a 48%. He needed the grades to stay in athletics so we convinced him to try and seduce her. Oddly enough, he was successful. He had stayed after class one day to get tutored. As she was leaning over his desk, he leaned over and started making out with her. Funny to see that she was desperately kissing him back. But, she didn't notice that I had left my phone in the corner of the room recording the whole thing. That night, I typed up a fake article for the paper with the headline "Extra Credit from Mrs. Anaya" explaining how she was having relations with her students. On the cover was a picture of them kissing and she freaked when I went to her class that morning to show her a preview. I didn't really publish it, but having her think I was going to was enough to get me and my friends 100% on everything the rest of the school year.

Those were just a few of the many crazy things my friends and I did together. Quite the delinquents we were, but we had *fun*. Why the change of heart and the urge to have me erased? I suddenly saw my flat-screen TV on the wall turn on. Nothing was on the screen, except black and grey static. The kind that appeared when there was no channel found. I looked around to see if Lennox and Tristan had come in, but I was alone. I set the picture frame back on the dresser and got up off my bed.

From static, the screen suddenly turned blue. Then the corner of the screen read PLAY. An image came on. There were people sitting at a table in a room I didn't recognize. As I looked closer at the faces on screen, I made out my friends. Red, Clemont, and Nolan were on one side of the table, sitting across from Satchel. It felt strange to Satchel again. Even if he wasn't in person directly in front of me, something about him now gave me an unsteady feeling. It must've been seeing him combust into flames. What was I watching?

Satchel was dressed in a white hospital gown while my friends wore regular clothes. Was I watching footage from security cameras from the hospital Satchel was in? I had to be. What else could this be? The angle sure looked like it. It was focused on the table without moving anywhere else. Clemont was the first to speak. "You guys, he's not going to go for it. He's known Zanniel the longest. He's like a hero to him."

Satchel scoffed. "The rest of you are here, aren't you?" He leaned forward on his elbows. "Look," he continued, "if he knows Zephyr as well as you say, then he knows exactly why we're here. Zephyr's no hero. That parasite should've been the one that hung himself."

"I understand your pain—" started Clemont but he was cut off by Satchel, who slammed his fists on the table, making the others jump.

"YOU DON'T KNOW MY PAIN!" shouted Satchel.

Clemont waited a few seconds before continuing. He seemed to choose his words carefully now. "Executing Zanniel will bring more complications than it will solutions.

"Then we deal with those complications when they occur."

No one said anything for a few beats. Then two more people came in and joined them in the table. One was Jason dressed in black scrubs, followed by Tristan in regular clothes. They sat in silence. Tristan drummed his fingers on the table. "This isn't weird at all," he said. "Now can you tell me why you dragged me here?"

"Okay," started Jason, "you know Satchel, right? Fletcher's brother?" Tristan didn't answer. Jason looked around at the others then continued. "Well, he's been locked up in here since Fletcher's incident. That's why we didn't see him at the funeral."

"Congratulations. Can I go now?" He stood up off his chair before Jason stopped him. He put his hand on his shoulder and gestured for him to sit back down. Tristan shrugged him off.

"What would you say," continued Jason, "if we had a plan to make our lives smoother?"

"That's evading. Can you just tell me why I'm here so I can get on with my day?"

"Fine," said Satchel, "straight to the point? You got it. You and your friends are going to get me out of here and you're all going to help me put Zephyr six feet under."

Tristan looked around at the others. "That's insane. Why would I help you do that? Why would *any* of you help him do that?"

"Zanniel's done more bad than good," said Nolan. "Just like we could've prevented Fletcher's death, we could prevent others from going through the same."

"So, you guys think killing him is the way to go?"

Such hypocrites! They were all there that morning and if they really wanted to stop me publicizing that article, they could've. Red spoke up. "I get it. Okay? Murder is wrong. And if we get caught, we'll be in deep shit for the rest of our lives."

"Which is why we *won't* get caught," barked Jason. "We just need to make sure we're all on the same page. That includes you, Tristan."

"This is ridiculous," said Tristan. "Whose idea was this?"

"Satchel presented us the stratagem," answered Clemont, "but, we've all had this feeling in the back of our minds since Fletcher's departure. All Satchel really did was bring our loathing to light."

"I moved my rehearsal dinner up," said Jason. "It'll give us just enough time before he's gone for good."

"And do what, Jason? Just show up at his place and start butchering him?"

"Of course not. We get him from his place and take him up to an old storage unit my parents own in Tijeras. They'll never find him."

Tristan chuckled. "I'm sorry. Last I checked, this was the psychiatric ward of this hospital. In other words, they keep crazy people locked up. If you guys are seriously taking orders from the detained, then you're all just as crazy."

"Zephyr killed my brother," snapped Satchel, "a life for a life don't you think?"

"What is wrong with you? Zanniel didn't *kill* Fletcher. He hung himself. His decision, not Zanniel's. How is killing him going to bring your brother back?"

"If Zephyr was never in the picture," said Satchel with anger riding in his voice, "this never would've happened. It's not fair that he gets to live out his perfect life in Kentucky while we're all left here to suffer the mess he left behind!"

"Fletcher's *dead*, Satchel," snapped Tristan, "let him rest in peace."

Satchel threw himself across the table, taking swings at Tristan. Red and Jason held him back. Satchel grunted in anger. "You're just like him!"

"Maybe I am. But, I know my place thanks to Zanniel. You guys can blame him all day for whatever you want, but he was a damn good friend and you guys know it! Jason would've probably overdosed and died had it not been for Zanniel. Nolan got his spot on varsity basketball freshman year 'cause of him. Clemont got out of his comfort zone and so did Red with Zanniel's help. Not to mention, we all would've been nobodies in high school had it not been for him!"

Damn, I was touched in a strange kind of way. Tristan stood up for me while the others didn't listen to reason. He saw the good in me while the others just chose to see the bad. "Get in my way," warned Satchel, "and you'll have the same fate as that asshole."

"Don't threaten me," retorted Tristan, "unlike you, I can just walk right out of here." With that said, he turned and started walking toward the exit.

"Wait," said Nolan, "you're not going to go tell him are you?"

"There's nothing to tell," said Tristan as he turned around. "There's no way you guys can get away with something like this. Some friends you guys are for even considering. Wait, no. Scratch that. You don't deserve to be addressed as Zanniel's friends, friends don't go around killing each other." Just as he left, the screen went back to the static before shutting off.

Tristan's last line, it amazed me that it's exactly how I would've said it. Is that why he's in Limbo? Because he chose not to tell me about their plan? Or was there more? He did ask what they planned to do with me. I looked around half expecting to see either Lennox or Tristan in my doorway. They weren't; I was alone. I thought back to what I just watched. Unbelievable how easily they were convinced about killing me. Had they no guilt? Tristan was the only one that really had my back and it cost him his life. But did he really? I wanted to believe that but from what I just watched, I believed otherwise. How long did he know about this?

I stood up and went out to the hallway that overlooked the living room. Lennox and Tristan were sitting on the couch conversing with each other. They didn't notice my presence. Should I say something to Tristan? Bring up what I just watched? I could, I mean, what else could I do now besides ask questions?

I made my way down the stairs and joined their company. Lennox was giggling at something. Were these two flirting? She saw me get close and straightened her face. "I didn't know Jason ran for homecoming court." There was a picture of Fletcher, Jason, and I with our crowns after homecoming coronation in her hands. Was she snooping around?

"Yeah, well," I answered, "there's a lot of things you don't know about Jason. Like the fact that he's a murderer."

She sighed. "He didn't kill you. He was at the dinner with me all the while the others went for you."

She was defending him? "He plotted to kill me. Just because he didn't physically do anything he's suddenly innocent? Don't forget, the only reason you had that rehearsal dinner that particular night was all in ties to going after me."

She stared at me for a few beats before speaking. "Jason loved me."

That was the best she got? "Oh, I'm so sure. Funny how he never even mentioned you *until* your little rehearsal dinner."

I struck a nerve. Even Tristan felt the new tension in the air. "That was a low blow. Where is this coming from?" He was right about the low blow. Lennox didn't really have anything to do with my friend's sick intentions. My attention really should be focused on Tristan.

"Your little meeting. At the hospital. Why didn't you tell me?"

He didn't answer me. He just stared at me. The sour look on his face told me that he had something to say, but he was choosing not to. I guessed I'd have to shake him up a little. "You wanted me dead, too. Didn't you?" I said it as a question but it was more of a statement. His silence reassured my accusation.

"You felt their pain, too," I continued, "you wanted me gone but you didn't want any part of it. You knew they would succeed in breaking Satchel out. Knowing what they were going to do, but by not doing *anything* about it, you kept your hands clean. That's why you kept quiet, wasn't it?"

He still didn't answer. "Wasn't it?!" I repeated. I made him jump. Looking closely at his face, tears began falling down his cheeks.

He stood up. "Fletcher was my friend, too!"

"We *all* loved Fletcher!" I countered, "no one knew that our little stunt was going to cost him his life. *You* didn't do shit to try and stop it from happening!"

"I know I didn't!"

"Why didn't you then? Why did you go through with it if you knew it was wrong?"

"Because you told me to!" He sat back down and put his face in hands. He was sobbing now. Because I told him to? What was that supposed to mean?

"All any of us ever did," he cried through his hands, "was to please you! We knew better than to tell you 'No' to anything! Not only did all of us respect the famous Zanniel Zephyr, but we were scared, too!"

"Scared?" I was confused. "Scared of what? I *made* each and every one of you!"

"Exactly!" He stood up. His face was wet and his freckles looked ten shades darker. "It was our *obligation* to keep you happy. Anything you ever asked of us, the smallest of demands, we always did it. The only one that tried stopping you that day was Nolan and you broke his nose!"

"So, it's my fault that you guys got upgraded lives? I didn't *force* anyone into anything. You all acted of your own free will. If you felt threatened by me, that's your own fault!" How did this turn into an argument? Yes, I unleashed my accusations onto Tristan but he confirmed them himself. The only reason I had so much power over my friends was because *they* allowed me to have it.

"Yes, we felt threatened! Could you blame us? And as far as not telling you, they didn't mention it again. A few days passed and they didn't bring it up so I thought it was all a hoax. Part of me did want you gone, I admit it. But, when you said you saw Satchel at UNM, I knew that the plan was still in motion and that they were coming for you. I came to my senses and knew that having you killed wasn't what I wanted. That's why I freaked and rushed over here to try and prevent it."

So, Tristan wanted me dead, too. Talk about spineless. "How could you act so normal around me? Knowing what was going on behind my back, you hypocritically smiled at me and pretended that everything was okay. How could you do that to me, *friend?*"

"Because you were leaving, dude! You gave us these perfect lives but the only reason they *were* perfect is because you were still there! Look how freshman year at UNM went: yes, we were all still close but not nearly as much as we were in high school. We're *hopeless* without you, Zanniel. Red and Nolan only made the basketball team because they were part of the Savage Seven. Clemont stopped doing sports and focused on his studies and look what happened? He hardly hung out with us anymore. There went his popularity out the door. How long before that started to happen to the rest of us?"

"What am I, your babysitter? Why should it be my responsibility whether you guys would be successful with or without me? The whole point of your successful lives back at Rio was so that you guys could mature and handle any life challenge that got presented to you! Is that another reason you wanted me dead, too? Because I was leaving you on your own?"

He sighed in frustration. "That's unrelated. My point is I know I did wrong by not telling you and by not doing anything to stop Fletcher's death. I just… ugh! I'm sorry!"

Just as he said "sorry" all the lights in the house turned on. The lamps, hallway lights, ceiling lights, everything. I looked around and so did the others. It was quiet except for our heavy breathing from the argument. Just after a few seconds of them turning on, the light bulbs in everything started exploding one by one. Along with the bulbs, the windows began being blown in, shattering glass in every direction. Tristan and I jumped while Lennox gave small shrieks with every pop and smash. As fast as my house lit up, it was dark now. Darker than before.

There was a breeze. Lennox's hair started flowing in front of her face. None of us moved, we stood frozen with anticipation as to what was going to happen next. The walls began cracking. The glass shards that fell on the floor began to rise and float to the ceiling. My first thought was for us to get out before my house decided to collapse on us.

I headed toward the door and the others followed without question. Once out in my driveway, we saw there was a circular motion of the fog surrounding the house. This felt just like Axel's departure. Tristan stood closest to the door, just staring at it. He then started walking back toward the house. What was he doing? Should we leave? Go find something else? Or did something need to happen here just like things had been done in the past?

"What's he doing?" Asked Lennox.

"Tristan!" I shouted. He didn't respond. I made my way over to retrieve him before something happened. But, when I reached for him, the familiar feeling of nothingness crept back to me. Just like Axel, my hand went through Tristan's arm. I couldn't do anything anymore. This was his time.

I pulled back and walked backwards toward Lennox. With nothing left to do, all we could do is watch and wait to see what Tristan's fate was. The wind circling us got faster. I was staring at Tristan before a flash blinded me. I closed my eyes shut and turned away. A few seconds passed before I tried to open them. When I slowly opened them, I was in awe. Tristan was wearing white all over. His jeans were white as well as his shoes. His sleeveless flannel turned from a black and red pattern to white and grey. He looked to be glowing slightly. He turned to face us and had a shocked look was on his face. Shocked, but with a slight smile. His freckles were more pronounced and his brown hair was combed cleanly up then to the side. His body didn't seem to feel the wind anymore, nothing was moving in correspondence with it.

He gave me a side smile and a wave before turning around again. The door shut behind him as he slowly walked inside. The top of the house started disintegrating. And before anything else happened, there was another bright flash. I didn't need to open my eyes to see. I knew what Tristan's fate was. I'm glad he didn't burn like Satchel. He didn't do anything wrong but try so hard to keep up with me and my ego. Tristan was gone and I had the odd feeling that he and I weren't going to the same place. But, this was Limbo after all and I couldn't say I knew how it worked.

When I opened my eyes, the wind had subsided and my house was gone. The only thing left was a dove picking at something on the ground. It looked around for a bit before flapping its wings and taking off.

Good bye, Tristan.

XVIII

Fates

As I stared at the dove fly away, I wondered: what will become of *me*? Yes, I feel all the regret, pain, and hurt that I caused others *now*. But, not when I was alive. Was it too late for me? Had my fate already been decided and I was just wandering Limbo waiting to see how it played out? Can I change it? Many questions, no one to answer them.

I was so lost in thought that I didn't notice Lennox had started walking away. I couldn't see that good through the fog that still surrounded us, but I could make out Lennox's big red bow on the back of her blonde hair. Where was she going? Seriously, as far as I was concerned she was just wandering astray. Last I checked, she was the one following *me*. When did the roles change?

"Where are you going?" I called out.

"Don't worry about it," she answered.

I chuckled. "Wow. Wonder where I've heard that one before." Why was she mad at *me*? I've done nothing but tell her the truth about Jason and the truth about her allegations about me causing a chain reaction. I picked up my pace and walked up next to her. She didn't look my way, nor did she change her pace.

"You're right," she said. I was right? About what? I'd told her so many things; I would assume she meant all of them.

"About?"

"Jason. He never loved me."

Ugh. Was this really what was bothering her? Chicks. "Jason *did* love you."

"Don't humor me. There's no need to."

She was so stubborn. I wanted to play punch her shoulder to loosen her up a bit. Though she wouldn't feel it and she probably wouldn't find it playful, so I restrained my urge. "Jason was smart not to bring you around me."

She stopped short and crossed her arms over her chest. "How?"

She wanted me to explain. Of course, she wanted to be humored. Who was she kidding? "You've been around me long enough. You really think Jason would want you around that?"

She stared at me wanting more. "He was smart to keep you away," I admitted, "plus, even if it did have to do with killing me, he proposed to you. That's big for Jason. In high school, he was all about that drink-and-party scene. He had girlfriends here and there but they were never serious. I was unsure as to whether his engagement was even legitimate."

She was convinced. I could tell on her face. "Murder and plotting to kill me aside, Jason was the only one of my friends that I didn't change. He had a life and a backbone all his own. The only thing I tried to change were his drinking habits. I ridiculed him for being the only guy on the school dance team, but that didn't stop him. Our dance team was good shit—they won state twice. Not that I ever admitted that to him."

I was rambling now. Even Lennox could tell that I was getting off topic. But, from the looks of it, she liked hearing about Jason. "My point is, Jason never felt like he had to prove himself with me. He wasn't a 'robot' I programmed. He was always himself no matter what others thought." She still didn't say anything. Then I wondered. "Hey, if you're so in love with Jason, why didn't you two start dating when you first met?"

She played with the ends of her hair with one hand while she answered. "I felt a connection that night at his party. But, I was too involved with cheer that I didn't make room in my life for anything else.

But, I do wonder: had he and I actually started dating after that night, would I have ever even *done* any of my devious acts?"

"I..." I tried, "can't answer that. But, how did you get away with cleaning out all those men without getting caught? How long did you even do that for?"

She smiled lightly. "Seven months until I crossed Jason's path that night. It was easy, but I was always scared out of my mind. Sometimes my hair would be black, others red. Sometimes it was up, others down. I wouldn't wear the same outfit twice within a months' time. But, I always found a way to match a hair bow to whatever I wore."

We started walking again. "I knew what I was doing was wrong. I knew I couldn't survive on doing these things forever, and I knew stealing was wrong. I was just desperate for money. I take back what I said before about you being the reason things happened this way. You're right, I can't control what happens to me but I can control how I react. Everything that happened to me was my own doing, no one else.

"Switching topics," she continued, "I don't mean to sound sexist in any way, but your role at your high school was typically that of a *girl*. I mean, every school has a mean girl, or girls, that think they own everything and everyone. No one ever really hears of that being *boys*. Unless, it's the bad boys who just cause trouble and fail at everything. But, you were a leader, not only to your friends, but to your whole school."

How did we get from arguing, to apologizing, to making small talk? Talk about strange. But, at least she owned up to being wrong. "Not sexist," I clarified. "But a little stereotypical."

She smiled. After a few more steps, I could see buildings through the fog. We were back in downtown. I wondered if this was where Lennox was going to cross over? I had no way of knowing for sure. But, I was anticipating it. The streets were just as empty as before, and it was dead silent except for my footsteps and Lennox's heels.

I'm not sure what to do now. I doubt that any of the doors were unlocked now. Even then, what's there to find? *I'm* not the one who died here, Lennox did. Then I thought of something. "Hey, what hotel did you die at?"

My question threw her off. "Ummm… the Albuquerque Home Style Suites, the one that's connected to the convention center."

I got excited suddenly. "Where I first met you?"

"I guess?" She shook her head. "Why the sudden interest?"

"I think we need to go there. Look what happened with all of the others; they were all in the places they died when they crossed over."

"And where did you die?" Damn. I just realized I never actually told her anything about my death. She heard parts of what happened from Satchel and Tristan, but I never willingly opened up about my death the way the others had.

"I woke up here in a storage unit," I said in a low voice, "Satchel must've left my body to rot there after he was done with me."

She nodded. She looked like she wanted to talk more about it but she just started walking. As we passed the buildings, I looked at my reflection. How did I end up here? I wondered. I had boyish good looks, except my eyebrows. I had brains, confidence, good physique… Did I take all that for granted? Did others hate me because I had these factors?

As I looked at my reflection, I saw a masked figure just like those who attacked me standing across the street. I stopped short and whipped my head around. Nothing. I then heard metal scraping behind me, the kind of noise you hear when you sharpen a knife. I quickly turned around. Still nothing. Was I imagining things? Was I losing it?

I shook off the creepy feelings and kept walking. In no time, Lennox and I arrived at the spot where we first met. The only thing missing was Axel, but he was in a better place. The encounter seemed so long ago. I wondered how long ago exactly, because I wasn't sure how time was measured in Limbo. Not that it mattered, it'd just be satisfying to answer at least one question. Lennox stopped in front of the building and looked up at the roof. I don't remember past my attack, but Lennox remembered everything clearly. Wonder what that was like? Replaying the events of your death over and over in your head? That must be what she was doing now. Why else would she stare blindly at this building?

Before I could say anything, she walked to the front door. I followed close behind. She paused for a moment at the door before opening it. She pulled the handle and the door swung open. She looked back at me for reassurance then went inside. The lights were all off and it was just as quiet as it was back when we were at my old school. I didn't think I'd ever been to this hotel. It seemed elegant with a giant crystal chandelier in the center of the room, marble walls throughout, and a staircase behind the reception desk that led up to the first floor, then branched off in two opposite directions to the upper levels. The rooms had maroon colored doors and the building had five floors, not including the roof level.

Lennox walked straight past the reception desk and began climbing the stairs. There were elevators on either side of us. But, I had a feeling they weren't running right now. She walked with a pace of familiarity; like she knew exactly where she needed to go.

"Do you mind," I told her, "letting me know where you're going before taking off? You keep doing this, and chasing others isn't really my thing."

"I'm going to the last place I was alive," she responded, "my rehearsal dinner."

For a second, I forgot that I was supposed to *be* at this dinner of hers. Had Tristan gotten to me before Satchel and the others, I would've climbed these stairs alive. I followed her up to the fifth floor. She turned left and headed down a long hallway with no rooms. The hall was dark but as it started to curve, it was illuminated. As we continued walking, there lights hung up on the ceiling. The kinds of lights to see hung around houses and trees during Christmas season. Kind of tacky in my opinion but it had a nice touch, I guess. On the walls, there were vases hung every ten feet or so. The flowers inside were none that I'd ever seen before. They were red, but the petals were strange curled loops that looked like they were too big for itself and they were scrunched together. "What are these?"

"Cockscomb flowers," she called back, "aren't they elegant?"

No, I thought to myself. They reminded me a little of the Golgi apparatus structure we learned in biology. Only with more curves. "Were they all out of roses?"

She turned and shot me a disapproving look. I'm assuming she was the one who picked them out. There were double doors at the end of the hall with a plaque above them that read "Ballroom D." She paused at the doors with her hands on the handles. Was it locked? Or was she holding on for dramatic effect? She took a deep breath and pulled them open.

Inside, it kept similar decorations as those in the hall. The room was illuminated by the same kinds of lights above the ceiling. There were about twenty round tables with red overlays and about ten chairs per table. The same freakish-looking flowers from the hall served as a centerpiece in each table. Around those were upside down wine glasses for each chair. There was a long rectangular table toward the end with more seats, which I could only assume was for the engaged and those who were involved in the wedding. On the back wall was a large picture of Lennox in Jason's arms on some train tracks. Jason looked happy with a cheesy smile. You think he would've shaved the patch of hair under his bottom lip. But no. He always kept it the same since I first met him. His black hair was combed up in spikes and his skin tone looked a little pale. Lennox had her hair up and had in what looked like a big black bow behind her blonde locks.

I started to think back to our freshman year at UNM and how Jason and I began losing connection. I was a journalism major and he was going for health-related fields so we didn't really have classes together. I did basketball and he stuck with dance. I would go to some of his parties still, but it wasn't always a direct invite. Tristan would often come to me asking if I was going to such and such party that I was unaware of. He didn't reach out to me nor did I to him. I wasn't sure if we were even on any of each other's social medias anymore. Funny how we went from best friends to complete strangers.

Then I began to think out loud. "Did Jason know about your little scams?"

She smiled and gave a soft chuckle. "Yes. He did. I thought he would be ashamed or mad or…something other than okay. But he just laughed. Told me that we all had our skeletons in the closet somewhere. Shared with me the delinquent side of him that he had in high school in an attempt to make me feel better."

…Did he mention me at all? The one who saved his life from almost drinking himself to death? The one who upped his popularity status and helped him pass math? "He ever mention me?" I sounded selfish for asking, but how could I not? I had a big influence on his high school career. He was bound to mention me *sometime*. Wasn't he?

She stared at the tables as she thought for a second. "Not directly. He had mentioned that one of his friends killed himself his senior year. He also said he was part of an infamous group others called 'Savage Seven.' Now that I think about it, he did mention once that he was tired of being a robot. I didn't know what he meant by that back then. But, he did say he was tired living by others' standards. *Now* I know that all of that was aimed at you."

I didn't know what to make of that. I didn't answer her. "Jason blamed my friends," she continued, "said Trinity and Destiny should've been more focused on the stunt." That last part was uncalled for but I saw his point. I didn't realize until just now how distant Jason and I actually got. Shame, we used to be close.

But, looking around at the fancy decorations, Jason really went all out on this wedding. Regardless if this entire thing was a hoax, he got the best things money could buy. But, did I not know Jason at all anymore? None of this was his scene. Since when was he about this life? Jason wasn't one to throw weddings, he crashes them. Had Jason's picture not been on the wall, I would've been clueless as to whose wedding this was.

Lennox walked around the room stroking the tables as she passed. I heard sniffling coming from her direction. Ugh, more tears. "Did I deserve this?"

"What do you mean?"

Her voice cracked. "Death. I mean, from what you know about me, did I deserve to die? Finally, when my life seems to get back in order, it just ends in the blink of an eye. I believe in karma, but I don't think death was the way to serve it."

She asked about herself but I was focused on me. I don't think *I* deserved to die. Sure, I'd done some harsh things to others, manipulated authority, and used many tactics to get my way. But, so did other people! Why was having a backbone such a bad thing? I chose to be a leader rather than a follower because I wanted my voice to be heard. I wanted people to know who I was and what I was capable of. Those who just took what they were given and never stood up for themselves didn't get anywhere in life. I thought I was teaching my friends to *not* be that way but they ended up hating me for it apparently.

"Well," I answered, "karma comes in different forms. You deserved punishment, that much is obvious. But, I will compliment the fact that you have balls. You know that? You could've been killed at any given time by any one of those perverts. Your little drug could've had no effect and you were already in a bad position by being alone and basically hopeless if you were to try and fight them off because of your injury."

I don't think I gave her the answer she was looking for. But at least I threw compliments her way. She pulled out a chair close by and took a seat. She looked down at the floor. "Do you think you deserved to die?"

Of course not! Leadership isn't a crime and neither is being ruthless. What is a crime is not taking control of your life. "Life is like a game of chess: you're either a king, pawn, or somewhere in between," I told her. "The way I saw it, I wore the crown, my friends were below me, and the rest of the world were pawns. If I didn't wear the crown, that meant someone else would. Why was I punished for not choosing to be like the rest?"

"Did you ever think it wasn't about your leadership, but the way you treated others?"

"No. Why should I have to censor my actions or words for the sake of sparing the feelings of others? If they're too sensitive for such material, then that's *their* problem. In the real world, people do things with the sole purpose of benefiting themselves. If we all stopped and took into consideration how others would feel about the things we did, then there would be no freedom of speech. Without that, we would just tell others what they want to hear."

"I'm sorry," she shook her head. "I don't know where you're going with this."

"My point is this: it's not my fault that people react the way they do when presented with unpleasant situations."

"I see your point," she said quietly, "but I don't agree with it."

"You don't have to. It's *my* point. Why is it so hard for others to understand that?"

She didn't answer. I heard metal scraping again and this time I was certain Lennox heard it as well because she gave a small gasp and whipped her head up. She stood up slowly and looked around. My eyes scanned the room but nothing looked out of place.

"I didn't die in here," said Lennox. She walked around the tables and headed for the exit toward the back of the ballroom. She was probably headed toward the roof where she was thrown off from. Was it so hard to tell me that? I followed her through the exit and up the stairs. We get to the top in a few steps. She stopped in front of the glass door that led to the roof. She opened the door slowly and stepped outside.

The outside had the same grim and foggy atmosphere all of Limbo had. She walked out closer to the ledge and I stayed close behind. She stopped at the ledge and put her hands over the bars that came up to her waist. She looked down and I did too. That was some drop. No one would've survived a fall from here. She was quiet. Was she still here or was she crossing over? I reached out to touch her and she turned to me before I did.

"Just making sure you're still here," I told her. She smiled. She turned her attention back toward the bottom of the building again. "Hey." I had a thought. "Technically you didn't die here either. You were thrown so I'm pretty sure you died when you hit the ground. Shouldn't we go back down to where I first saw you?"

She didn't respond but nodded. I headed back toward the glass door and assumed she was going to follow. I was back in the building and held the door open for her. "You coming?"

She didn't answer. She stayed where she was, looking down. "Lennox?" I tried. The wind picked up. I could see her hair and bow flowing in the same direction. The clouds were moving too. It was happening. The door forced itself to close, locking me inside. I tried to open it but it wouldn't budge. I pounded my fist hard on the glass. "LENNOX!"

The wind was circulating the entire building, just as it had with everyone before. Was she going to heaven? Or hell? I didn't know at this point. She wasn't innocent at all when it came down to her actions. She regretted everything and she knew how wrong it all was. But was that enough to grant her acceptance to heaven? Or was she deemed too corrupt for any chance of being saved? I stared hopelessly as the wind continued to stir. After what seemed like forever, a bright flash finally blinded me.

My eyes closed instantly. I found myself wanting her to go to heaven. To be with Tristan, Axel, and maybe even Fletcher. I didn't think she deserved hell, but that wasn't for me to decide. I slowly opened my eyes and found myself stunned. The wind was still whirling around but it looked more like a soft breeze. Lennox was still in the same spot as before. But the big red bow on the back of her head was now white. Her jacket, skirt, and heels were now a radiant white as well. She was going to heaven.

She turned her head back toward me and gave me a smile. The same kind of flawless smile both Axel and Tristan had done. She looked divine. As happy as I was that she was crossing over, this also meant that I was now completely alone in Limbo. Everyone else had their destinies set. I was the only one left here. At least, that's what I *wanted* to believe. I keep hearing scraping noises. The last one I heard, Lennox had heard it as well. But with her soon to be gone, there was no one for reassurance.

She turned back around but looked up to the sky rather than down. Another bright flash appeared and I knew she was gone. What now? Where was I to go? What was I to do? I never needed guidance or directions but they would be appreciated if given right now. I slowly opened my eyes and wasn't surprised to see a white dove flying into the sky. Well, I guess this is goodbye, Lennox.

Suddenly, everything outside went pitch black. Darker than anything I'd seen here. I squinted and leaned closer to see if I could see what was going on, but it was hard to make out anything outside. The lights weren't on inside but it was brighter inside than outside. What was happening? Then a figure came into view as they pressed their face on the other side of the glass. I screamed as I saw a hooded figure wearing the same mask Satchel was when he killed me. The white mask with dark holes for eyes and mouth crossed out in duct tape that I last saw when I was alive had me screaming out in fear. I stepped backwards and stumbled down the stairs.

The scarier part was that I *felt* the pain of falling. For the first time since I'd woken up here, I physically felt this. Once I landed at the bottom of the stairs, I slowly got up holding on to the rail on the side of the stairs for support. I limped to the door that would lead me back to the ballroom where the rehearsal dinner was held. What was going on? Why was I feeling things *now*? I had no idea why nor how but I needed to escape.

Inside, the ballroom was still dimly lit with the lights in the ceiling. I kept going toward the exit before I collapsed from the pain. I turned around to see if I was being followed; I was. Kind of. The figure stood at the end of the room. Motionless, the figure seemed to be frozen, looking at my direction. Who was under the mask? Better yet, *what* was under the mask? The lights started to flicker and I heard thunder roll in the distance. On either side of me, the walls looked like they were leaking blood. Or *some* kind of red substance. Only, it wasn't leaking from the ceiling down, it was from the ground up. The centerpiece flowers combusted into flames. Flames that twirled and danced all the way up to the ceiling. They looked like flame pillars. The room now had such a red glow from everything going on that it made the masked figure look more menacing and terrifying.

The figure reached behind it and pulled out a large scythe and grasped it firmly with both hands. Oh shit, I thought to myself. I'm going to hell.

XIX

Anguish

No. No, no, no, no, no, no, NO!!! This couldn't be happening. Was I that evil that I belonged in hell? Was I just as bad as Satchel was? To share the same fate with that psychopath meant that he and I were equals. But we were not! Why was this happening to me?

The masked figure started taking steps toward me. I pushed through the pain from falling down the stairs and pulled myself up. I tried to run with minimal success. I quickly made my way into the long hall that would take me back to the main staircase. The flower decorations that were lined up on the walls had combusted into bright flames as well. Everything was so hot around me. I could feel myself starting to sweat.

I had to get away. I wasn't sure where I could go. Every landmark I had encountered had disintegrated into nothingness. The only place that came to mind was the storage unit. But, was I safe there? Was that where I was meant to go? I couldn't think straight. All I could focus on was to try to escape. I heard a scraping noise behind me. I looked over my shoulder and saw the masked figure running its scythe across the wall, tearing it open and revealing more blood-like substance. Just like the ballroom, it was leaking up instead of down.

I made it to the stairs and started heading down. I looked down over the stairs. The lobby looked the same as it had when I first arrived. I wasn't sure if the masked figure was right behind me. I didn't want to look back. I didn't want to believe that this happening to me. Part of me thought it was pointless to try and escape. But, another part of me believed I *could* escape whatever this was. The masked figure did have a scythe but I was already dead. It wasn't like he could kill me again.

After two flights of stairs, I realized my legs didn't hurt anymore. I wasn't sure why or how but I had no time to question it. I decided to take a detour in one of the hotel rooms. I wasn't sure if they were locked or not but I took my chances. I headed for room 315 and to my surprise, the door opened. I let myself in and closed the door behind me. The room looked normal. A bed, a closet, bathroom and balcony. I went to the closet and attempted to hide. It probably wasn't the smartest idea to stay in a hotel whose fifth floor was on fire, but I had to try *something*.

As I touched my legs and the rest of my body, my fingertips felt like they tingled. It was as if was I feeling things for the very first time. Strange, but how did this work? I hadn't felt a thing the whole time in Limbo. Was there an on-and-off switch? And where did the pain I felt from falling earlier even go? Was physical pain temporary now?

I heard the door open and my body stiffened up. I heard footsteps and something being dragged along the floor. That masked figure was here. I kept completely still and quiet. I was probably making a fool of myself. This attacker probably knew I was in here. I had locked the door yet this thing let itself in like nothing had happened.

A few moments passed and I heard nothing. I kept still. I knew how these types of situations worked. I'd seen them happen plenty of times in movies. The killer stalks around and makes it seem like they've left the premises. When the victim feels safe, they come out of hiding only to find that the killer never left. I wasn't about to do that. I was staying in here if I wasn't forced to go out.

The silence was nerve-racking. I pressed my ear against the closet door to try and hear better. I heard nothing on the other side, no movement or any sound. The silence was suddenly broken by the scythe breaking through the closet door. The blade was just inches from my face that I was surprised it missed me. I looked closely at the rusted blade, full of scrapes, dirt and what looked like dry blood. The scythe got pulled out and I stayed where I was.

I heard the scythe break through the closet door again behind me. Missed *again*. Then a third time above my head. Was this attacker missing on purpose? Just toying with me? Just then, the scythe broke through again, this time piercing my left shoulder I had pressed up on the door. I let out a scream as the blade ripped through my skin. I could see blood running on the side of the door and down to the floor. I was *bleeding*. How was I bleeding?! I wasn't even alive! Nothing was making sense anymore.

The scythe got pulled back out after a few seconds. I pressed my hand over my wound to cover the bleeding. The door swung open and the masked figure looked down to me. "What do you want!?" I screamed. The attacker didn't answer. Instead, it pulled me up by my sweater vest and brought me to my feet. I stared at the mask. It looked just like the one my friends were wearing that night. As I stared through the dark eyeholes, a black snake crawled out of the left eye and slithered down its body. What *was* this thing? It had a human shape but that definitely wasn't a human beneath the mask.

The figure grabbed onto one of the gloves it was wearing with the other hand while still holding me. The glove slid off and the hand that was revealed looked like it was burning. It reminded me of the bark of a tree log you see burning in a fire place. The outer part was black and lumpy and through the cracks was a red faint glow. I tried to pull away, but then the attacker pressed its burning hand onto my face.

I screamed out in pain as I felt an intense burn taking place on the right side of my face. Not only could I hear a sizzle, but I saw smoke emanating from where my face met the hand. I kicked and squirmed but the attacker didn't budge. I closed my eyes as I screamed at the top of my lungs. I felt my body lifted off the floor and before I knew it, I was being thrown across the room. My body was throbbing and I felt the room spinning. I felt myself being picked up again and this time I was thrown through the glass door at the end of the room landing me on the outside balcony.

I didn't move. What was the point of fighting? I had no chance of even defending myself. My face felt like it was on fire, my body throbbed in pain, my arm was bleeding me dry… What else? As if on cue, I heard footsteps coming my way but I still didn't move. I felt myself lifted off the floor. I slowly opened my eyes and saw the masked attacker holding me up. With a small shove, it threw me over the ledge. I was falling from the third floor. That was enough to kill someone. But, would I die? Would I be put out my misery now?

I felt my body hit the ground. I couldn't find words to explain the pain I felt. No one would be alive after being attacked this way. But I was already *dead*. Could I die again? I wanted to. At least I wouldn't feel any more pain. I wanted all physical feeling to escape my body the way it was when I first woke up. The pain was too much to handle. I decided to just lie here. Maybe, if I lay here long enough, something might happen. Maybe the attacker would leave me alone. But, unfortunately, I knew that wasn't going to be the case.

I wasn't sure if I had passed out or something, but I woke up feeling refreshed. I was lying on the concrete in front of the hotel I had been inside. I touched my bare shoulder and realized my wound was gone. I quickly got to my feet and inspected my body. Not a scratch on me. I ran to the glass doors of the hotel to see my reflection. As I looked at myself, I looked fine. Better than fine, I looked perfect. My bronze hair was done, my face had no burn, my shoulder had no cut, and my sweater vest had no blood or anything else on it. Did I imagine the whole thing? I looked around and saw the same foggy substance that surrounded everything.

So, what now? Everything seemed normal. Well, as normal as Limbo could be. But this time, I was alone, no more Axel, Satchel, Clyde, Tristan, or Lennox. They'd all crossed over and I was sure that it was my turn after Lennox, but here I was still. I wasn't entirely sure if Clyde had crossed over or if he had survived his incident; I didn't think too much about it. But where was the masked attacker? Downtown looked completely abandoned from the looks of things. Did it vanish? Move on? The isolation didn't bother me as much if it meant being away from that… whatever it was. I tried to open the doors to the hotel, but they were locked. I went back to the side of the building where I'd been thrown from. I looked up at the third floor of balconies but none of them had the glass shattered. They all appeared to be untouched. Hmmm…strange.

Maybe, just maybe, I was supposed to go back to the place where I had woken up at, the place I died. Thinking back to the others, they all crossed over when they got to the places that their deaths occurred. I decided to head back that way. As I walked, I realized that downtown *looked* the same, but it didn't *feel* the same. It felt darker, scarier. Part of that feeling probably came from the reminder that there was some human-like creature walking around wearing the same white mask with duct tape over the mouth that Satchel and the others wore when they came for me. But something felt different. I just wasn't sure what.

As I turned onto Central Avenue, I saw a flock of crows on the road. I stopped short. I don't recall animals being in Limbo? There were doves that appeared when someone crossed over to heaven and there was that one snake I had seen slither out of the attacker's mask. But this was strange. They had a sinister feel to them and I felt scared to get near them.

They're just *birds*, I told myself. I took a deep breath and proceeded toward my destination. When I got close, the flock of crows flew out in many directions into the foggy, hazy sky. When I passed the movie theater and got closer the train tracks, I heard a goat cry out behind me. I gave a small cry at the sound and when I turned around, a goat was standing in the middle of the road. It was standing in a spot I'd passed, but it wasn't there a few seconds ago. I stared at it half-expecting it to do something unusual or demented. Instead, it just cried out again.

I heard a train approaching. When I turned around, I came face to face with my attacker again. It swung its scythe at me but it barely missed as I threw myself on the ground and out of its way. I tried to crawl away quickly, but before I knew it, I felt the intensity of the blade penetrating the back of my right calf. I screamed out in pain as I felt myself being dragged backwards toward the train tracks.

I turned over on my back and saw the train passing behind my attacker. Only, it was moving about a hundred miles an hour. The attacker pulled the scythe out of my leg then threw it to the side. There was blood all around me from the fresh wound. The attacker picked me up with both hands and got me to my feet. I was turned around, made to face the passing train. I felt both of my hands restrained behind my back, and I felt one hand grab the back of my hair.

I could barely see my reflection in the silver coating of the train as it passed. I was being pushed forward. After a few steps, I was inches away from the train. I couldn't fight back, it was too strong and the pain from the cut on my leg had me unable to even stand on my own. I felt the back of my head being pushed forward. I tried to push back, but failed. This thing was going to destroy my head by pressing it on a moving train!

"NO!!!!" I pleaded. But, before I knew it, I felt the burning of metal scraping along the right side of my face. The attacker pressed it firmly as the train kept moving. The friction from the movement had me screaming in agony. I felt my body squirming and I thought my head was going to get completely obliterated. Would this train never end? I was hoping that the train would pass us so that the friction would end and I would get a break; trains weren't *this* long. But, it kept going and my face kept burning. It felt like I was shouting, but I don't think I made any noise.

After what seemed forever, I got lifted back. I was pretty sure half of my face was gone at this point. I was thankful I couldn't see it; if it looked as bad as it felt, that would be more pain all on its own. I felt my body being thrown to the ground. All I heard was ringing in my ears. If my right ear was in fact still connected to me. I felt my body trembling the way someone having a seizure would. What was going *on*? Where did my attacker go? I didn't have any energy to get up, I just lay there. After a few moments, I found myself rolling on my side. Then, I sat up with a jolt. I could move again.

There was no train in front of me. No attacker, not even the damn birds. I lifted my hand to touch my face and realized it felt normal. Did I imagine all of that? No. No way. I didn't just *imagine* all that pain. My leg looked fine, too. There was no blood anywhere nor a tear on my jeans. Ugh! What was happening? I got up and looked around. Everything was still. Downtown looked practically abandoned. Where did the attacker keep disappearing off to?

I turned around and kept going. This wasn't right. Frustrating part of it was that there was no one here to talk about it with. Not Lennox to nag nor Tristan to agree on whatever explanation I would come up with. I passed the train tracks and before I knew it, I was approaching the same chain-linked fenced I had climbed when I first woke up here. "Tijeras Self Storage" read the sign above. I climbed back over and headed back to the unit I came from: 58.

10, 12, 14 I passed. I was getting scared. What was going to happen once I was back inside? Would I finally cross over? 26, 28, 30… Was I going to heaven? Probably not. But, Lennox did. And she did some pretty messed up things. 42, 44, 46… Tristan did, too and he was basically another version of me. There had to still be *some* hope. 54, 56… 58. I stopped in front of the black garage-looking door. This was it. I grabbed the handle and swung it open. The door went up revealing the empty space. I went in and slid the door back down.

I let my eyes adjust for a moment and then walked to the center. Now what? Nothing was happening. Ugh! I placed my arms across my chest and started to think. Why was nothing happening? I was at the spot where I died, just like the others. Where was *my* big crossover scene?

It was quiet as quiet can be and the lack of change around me was getting unsettling. Did I need to do something else? Go somewhere else?

I saw a reddish glow coming through the bottom crack of the door from the outside. It was flickering. *Flames*, I thought. And then I realized it. I dropped to my knees as I began to hyperventilate. I had already crossed over. I was *in* hell. That's why the pain I felt would leave my body. This masked creature that was terrorizing me would cause me new pain, pain that would be enough to *kill* anyone. After I was done agonizing in pain, the cycle would repeat and new pain would come.

I saw this cycle happening but I hadn't realized it then. After Lennox crossed over, that's when I must've crossed over as well. *That's* why I felt physical pain now. *That's* why I'm being tortured by that creature. I wasn't entirely sure why it looked just like my attackers from the night I was killed. This cycle I was now in seemed to be in a continuous loop: I get attacked, feel pain and misery, then my body refreshes, and it repeats. This was my hell. I was more than positive that my attacker was on the other side of the door. He'd keep coming for me, torture me, I'd recover, and it would happen all over again.

I could feel tears running down my cheeks. Was I really that terrible when I was alive to deserve an eternity of endless pain and suffering? I'm sorry, Fletcher. I'm sorry, Tristan. I'm sorry to everyone else whose lives were affected by my actions. I knew apologizing wasn't going to get me anywhere. But, I still felt sorry. The door began sliding up slowly. Flames made their way in lighting up the room. The door opened all the way up, revealing the masked attacker. It held the door up with one arm and had a scythe in the other. I began sobbing.

The attacker slowly walked my way holding the scythe in both of its hands. He paused in front of me and watched me cry helplessly. The attacker rose the scythe above its masked head. This torture was never going to end. It would just reset itself and I would feel new pain each time. If I were alive, I would want to die so the pain would end. But I was already dead, death wouldn't come. I was forever to be this thing's toy, to play with my body in torturous ways.

I closed my eyes and let out a scream as the attacker swung the scythe in my direction. It was pointless to scream. But, I figured if I closed my eyes, it would soften the blow, make the slashing from the scythe less painful if I didn't see it open my skin. It didn't help at all. If anything, it only made the cut more painful.

XX

Awakened

BEEP… BEEP…

"He's waking up!"

"Shh…easy, big boy."

BEEP… BEEP…

Clyde slowly managed to open his eyes. All he saw at first was the blinding blur of the ceiling lights. He tried to lift his head but it felt like it weighed a ton. As his sight got more in focus, he looked around the room and saw familiar faces. He also saw the white bed sheets that covered his body and a few tubes and wires that were inserted into his forearms.

The beeping began to grow faster as Clyde started to move around. Clyde wanted to rip the tubes out, get the sheets off and get out of this strange place all together. His companions at the end of the bed carefully restrained him down while shushing him as an indication to relax. What happened? Last thing he remembered, he was chasing down some masked lunatic in a cement factory off the highway.

He looked anxiously around for the masked character. Did he escape? But, he remembers shooting him. Was he dead? "His memory will be a little fuzzy," said a tall brunette nurse that was writing something down on a clipboard. "I trust you two can help with that. His wounds are still very sensitive and the anesthesia might wear off. If he starts to get a little rowdy, please press the emergency button and the doctor will be right in.

"In the meantime, you can calm him down with some small talk and maybe get him to drink water to stay hydrated. I'll go collect his medicine that will help with his swelling." With a turn on her heel, she left the room. Clyde could barely breathe regardless of the oxygen mask he just realized he had on. He reached for it, but his wife, Destiny, held his hand down.

"Sweetie," she tried, "no, no, no. Leave that on." Destiny had her black hair up in a bun with her bangs over her tear-filled eyes. She had on a black strapless dress, a dress Clyde liked seeing her in but made him uncomfortable at the thought that other guys liked seeing her in it as well.

To her left was an old friend of Clyde's, CJ. He was wearing a black button up with his black hair slicked back and his rectangular-framed glasses were pressed up on the bridge of his nose. He still had all his piercings on his lips and ears which bothered Clyde in the sense that his appearance lacked professionalism. Both were dressed elegantly, thought Clyde. What was the occasion?

Of course! He just remembered the rehearsal dinner they were both going to. Clyde was supposed to go, but he got caught up with work so CJ went in his place. But, why was Destiny crying? Because he was in the hospital? He slowly removed the oxygen mask. "Ah can breathe," he assured before Destiny could protest. "Wu' happened?"

Destiny began sobbing as she tried to explain. "It's been a horrible night. Lennox killed herself, Clyde. She jumped off the hotel roof!"

Jumped off? No, no, thought Clyde, that didn't sound right.

"Remember that cat I was trying to catch?" Asked CJ. "The one I told you about that was going up and down New Mexico drugging guys and cleaning their wallets? Well, turns out Destiny's friend here was that same one."

"Lennox kept secrets," continued Destiny. "CJ tried to stop her from her suicide. But, I guess—I don't know. She must've felt too guilty or something. First that happens. Then I get news that you're in critical condition. I lost one of my best friends tonight. I was scared to death that I was going to lose you, too."

"Yeah, man" added CJ, "looks like all the time you spent at the gym actually paid off. The doctors said you had over twenty stab wounds on your back and abdomen. But, all that muscle you packed on prevented the knife from hitting anything major."

There was a faint vibrating noise. Destiny reached for her purse and pulled out her phone. "It's Trinity," she told Clyde. "I'll just be a minute." She leaned over and kissed him gently on the forehead and went out to the hall answering her phone. There was an awkward vibe in the room. Clyde stared at CJ intensely. Slowly, he started to remember everything that he encountered earlier. He thought he had dreamt everything, but there was no way. He couldn't explain how nor why, but the Limbo realm he had inhabited for a short time was definitely real.

CJ shifted uncomfortably at Clyde's stare. "What's up?"

Lennox didn't kill herself, Clyde thought to himself. CJ killed her. But how could he approach the situation without sounding insane? Clyde wasn't even *at* the rehearsal dinner. How could he back up his story? But he had to try. "You see 'er jump?"

CJ narrowed his eyes. "Yeah, man. I tried to stop her but—I don't know, guess she just felt too guilty or something like Destiny said."

"So…what? You jus' go up to 'er an' say ya know who she was?"

"Well, no, not like that. She left the dinner and headed to the roof and I followed her. I did say that I knew the things she'd been up to and that I was going to have to take her in for questioning."

"Alone?"

"Yes, *alone*. Everyone else was down at the dinner."

"'Ow convenient. Nobody can serve as a witness to yer alibi."

"*Alibi?*" CJ was getting defensive. "What are you getting at, man?"

CJ stood up and crossed his arms over his chest. Clyde wanted to get up, too. But he was hooked up to too many things. He thought it best to stay where he was. "Ya ever meet 'er before?"

"No, I hadn't."

"Yet, ya knew it was 'er?"

"I'm a detective, man. I have pictures, descriptions, whereabouts… What are you on?"

"I'm on to *you* righ' now. Y'xpect me to believe that Lennox jumped off the roof of the 'otel the night of 'er rehearsal dinner 'cause she felt 'guilty.'"

CJ scoffed. "Yeah, I do. That, or she probably got scared when she saw me and tried to escape."

"An' why would she be scared of you? Could it be 'cause maybe she got 'way from you that night in Belen when she stole yer car?"

"*Maybe,*" spat CJ. "That would just add on to the rest of her charges."

Clyde's mouth turned into a side grin. He knew CJ was lying and he was going to do everything he could to prove it. He kept hearing Lennox's words echo in his ear before he left Limbo. "*Please, Clyde,*" she had told him, "*for me, bring him to justice. I'm sorry for the crimes I committed, but you can't let him walk away from murder.*" CJ noticed the smile. "What's so funny?"

"Ya jus' agreed with me that she stole yer car. But, you jus' said ya hadn' met 'er before the dinner? Hmmm…not addin' up, is it?"

CJ chuckled. "*Okay,* nice word manipulation, Officer. You weren't even there tonight! What do *you* know?"

"Yer right. Ah wasn' there. But, what ah *do* know is Lennox didn' kill 'erself. You did. Also know that ya met 'er before. She took yer car an' emasculated you when she got 'way. But ya got yer revenge. Congratulations. Made sure she was dead so she wouldn' be out takin' no other man's pride."

CJ stared at Clyde in disbelief. Where was he getting all this information? He wasn't even at the dinner or in Belen the night Lennox got away. But that didn't matter to him. He stepped closer to Clyde so only he could hear. "I don't know what you think you're getting at here, man. But I will say this…"

He leaned forward and whispered in Clyde's ear, "Good luck proving it in court." He stood up straight and threw Clyde a smile. He reached into his pocket and pulled out a big red bow. The same bow Clyde had seen Lennox wearing in Limbo. CJ twirled the bow in his hands before pressing it to his nose, taking a deep inhale. He gave him a wink, then turned toward the door, returning the bow to his pocket. Clyde stared at him furiously as he exited the room without looking back. Clyde's heart rate monitor began racing. Destiny came in as she heard the machine.

"Hey, hey, hey," she told him as she placed her hands on his shoulders, "you're okay, babe. Just breath." But Clyde wasn't having it. He pulled off the wires attached to his arms and threw the blankets off, moving Destiny out of his way. "Clyde!" she shrieked.

He got up and pushed past her but only got to the doorway. Doctors rushed his way and tried to restrain him. Clyde tried fighting back but his body was too weak. "MURDERER!!!" he yelled before he felt a doctor grab his arm and inject him with a tranquilizer. He felt the room start to spin instantly and his body grew weak. The doctors placed him back on his bed and placed the oxygen mask back on him before he passed out.